"You are not the same, Marcella."

Roumayne flushed under Eugene Hugo's penetrating gaze. What was he trying to say? Could he possibly know that she wasn't really Marcella, that she was only an impostor?

She laughed nervously. "Two years in Paris would change any girl. You've changed, too, Eugene. But I—I still want to marry you."

"Really?" Eugene mocked. "Did it ever occur to you, Marcella, that I might not want to marry you? That I never wanted to marry you?"

Desperately, Roumayne's mind raced back to the conversations she had had with Marcella. Marcella had seemed so sure that Eugene wanted her. Well, it didn't matter how Eugene felt. Roumayne knew that somehow, she still had to get him to propose!

Other titles by

ROSEMARY CARTER

IN HARLEQUIN PRESENTS

Other titles by

ROSEMARY CARTER

IN HARLEQUIN ROMANCES

ROSEMARY CARTER

sweet impostor

Harlequin Books

TORONTO • LONDON • NEW YORK • AMSTERDAM
SYDNEY • HAMBURG • PARIS

Harlequin Presents edition published May 1979
ISBN 0-373-70783-5

Original hardcover edition published in 1978
by Mills & Boon Limited

CHAPTER ONE

ROUMAYNE MALLORY paused on the steps of the Supreme Court, and blinked her eyes against the dazzle of the sun. A crowd had gathered on the pavement. At sight of Roumayne a woman screamed, 'Murderess!'

There was a moment of silence, then other screams and shouts began, the sound rapidly swelling to an ugly roar. Defiantly Roumayne lifted her tawny-haired head and stared over the heads of the people, willing the legs which felt suddenly weak to remain steady.

'Don't mind them.' John Gorton had followed her through the doorway. 'They want their pound of flesh.'

'Don't they know I've been acquitted?' She turned to the lawyer, amethyst eyes bright with unshed tears.

'They do. But they don't like it. Come on, Roumayne.' A hand gripped her elbow and he steered her firmly and uncompromisingly through the crowd.

Once they had left the environs of the Court they were left alone. The streets of Johannesburg bustled with people too intent on their business to spare a glance for the middle-aged man and the small slender girl with the pale oval face which made her look so much younger than her twenty-two years. They did not know that she was Roumayne Mallory, the girl who for the past two weeks had been the centre of a court case which had made headlines.

When they came to Eloff Street, where John Gorton had his office, they stopped. 'So, Roumayne, it's all over.' He was smiling, quiet and kind as he had been through the traumatic weeks since she had been charged with manslaughter.

'Is it, Mr Gorton ...?' A despairing face was turned upward to his. 'You saw the crowd back there at the Court.'

His mouth tightened. 'I told you—they don't like it. But you must try not to let it worry you.'

'It won't be simple.' Her voice was unsteady. People know I was only acquitted for lack of proof. They'll still think I killed Jackie James.'

'That's true....' The kind face was troubled. 'That aspect of the matter concerns me too. If only we could have come up with some kind of evidence!'

'And if only the person hadn't been Jackie James,' Roumayne put in ruefully.

'That too. The accidental death of a popular pop star was bound to cause hysterics and headlines.'

'You believe me, don't you, Mr Gorton?' Despair tinged her voice.

'I've believed you all along, Roumayne.' The grey eyes were warm. 'And your friends, your real friends, will believe you too.' He paused, and when he spoke again his expression was thoughtful. 'I didn't see Dr Mason in court today.'

'Alec couldn't get away from the hospital.' The amethyst eyes clouded.

'He'll be as relieved as you are that it's all over. Now you'll be able to set a date for the wedding.'

'Yes.' Roumayne tried to smile. She could not let the lawyer know how hurt she had been by Alec's absence today.

'I must say goodbye now, Roumayne. I've an appointment.' He reached for her hand. 'Take care of yourself, my dear. And don't forget to invite me to the wedding.'

She watched him disappear in the traffic, a tall, thin, middle-aged man. The advocate had been the one who had defended her at court, but it had been the lawyer, John Gorton, who had helped her through the weeks of unhappiness and uncertainty. True, she had to pay for his services, and the final bill which faced her now was staggering, yet in addition to his legal expertise John Gorton had shown a warmth and kindliness which had sustained her through the time of trauma. A time which was over now.

Or was it?

Already the first editions of the evening newspapers were appearing on the pavements. 'Lack of evidence in pop star acquittal,' was one headline. Roumayne saw her picture below the big title letters. A bad picture, taken when she was unawares, it made her look the kind of person who might really have been guilty of the crime of which she had been acquitted.

Biting her lip, she turned her eyes from the newspaper and hurried to the bus stop. As she waited for the bus Roumayne felt as if every eye were on her, as if the thought of every person in the queue was, 'Jackie James would be alive today were it not for that girl's negligence.'

Home was in the flat-land of Hillbrow, two rooms on the tenth floor of a building near the hospital. The flat faced south, away from the sun, and the view from its windows was the façade of an equally tall and dreary-looking building. Normally she could not wait to get away from it. All week she looked forward to Sundays when she and Alec were both free and could go boating on the Vaal River. But for once, the quiet isolation of her own walls was a refuge.

Away from hostile eyes she could let her shoulders droop. She filled the kettle and put it on the stove. As she waited for it to boil she wondered when Alec would come: 'I need you,' she pleaded silently, feeling tears pricking at her eyes. 'All day I've needed you. Come to me, Alec. Put your arms around me, and I'll feel better. *You* know that I'm innocent, and nobody else matters.'

She was sipping her tea when the door-bell rang. With a cry of joy she put down her cup and ran to open the door.

'Alec, I've been. . . .'

The words died away at sight of the girl who stood in the hallway. 'I've nothing to say to the Press.' Her tone grew flat, and she was about to close the door when the girl took a quick step forward.

'I'm not from the Press.' She was smiling, an appealing, friendly smile. 'Please let me come in.'

'Who are you?' Roumayne looked at her doubtfully, wondering at the face which was somehow familiar. The smile and the words could be part of a trick. More than one reporter had taken advantage of her gullibility.

'My name is Marcella Du Toit.'

'The name means nothing to me.'

'Of course it doesn't.' Laughter bubbled in the girl's throat. 'Poor dear, you must be really exhausted after all you've been through, otherwise you'd have noticed it already.'

'I don't understand....' Roumayne's head was throbbing. The reason for Marcella's amusement escaped her.

'You will. May I come in?'

'Very well.' She stepped aside to allow her visitor into the flat. 'But I warn you, if you're from the Press, you'll have to leave.'

'I've told you—I'm not.' Still smiling, Marcella Du Toit stood watching her. 'You haven't spotted it, have you?'

Roumayne put a hand to her aching temples. 'Perhaps you'd better just tell me what you're talking about.'

'Where is there a mirror?'

'I beg your pardon?' Was this after all just a stunt to wangle a story from her? There could be a camera hidden in Marcella's handbag....

'A mirror—you must have one. In there?' She gestured toward the open door of the bedroom.

'Yes, but.... Hey, you can't go in there!' Roumayne's voice rose on a note of protest as her unexpected visitor made for the bedroom.

'No need to get uptight. You do have a mirror.' Marcella Du Toit beckoned as Roumayne followed her into the room. 'Come here,' she ordered. 'No, here. Right next to me.' And then, impatiently, as Roumayne frowned into the mirror: 'You see it now. Surely you must!'

'I don't know what you mean.' Roumayne's mind was only on how she could get this strange girl out of her flat.

'Impossible! It's staring you in the face—literally.' Again the bubble of laughter. 'You really don't see it?' She sighed. 'Okay, I'll spell it out. We could be twins.'

'Twins?' For the first time Roumayne consciously took in the mirror image. No wonder Marcella's face had seemed familiar. If she hadn't been so tired, so preoccupied, she would have noticed the likeness immediately. It really was striking: the same tawny-coloured hair, the same blue eyes, the same upturned noses. But twins? One face was pale and unhappy, the other was alive with colour and high spirits. In the light of this essential difference all other similarities appeared insignificant.

She glanced at the other girl. Marcella was watching her impatiently. 'Well?' she demanded.

'There *is* a likeness,' Roumayne conceded uncertainly.

'A likeness, she calls it. Jeepers! We're the split image of each other!'

'What of it?' It seemed useless to argue with this explosive stranger.

'At least we can talk, now that I've got you to see it.' Mischief leaped in Marcella's eyes. 'Let's go back to the other room. Was that tea you were drinking? I'm parched. Give me a cup, then we'll talk.'

Marcella drained two cups quickly, then began to speak. Roumayne sat quietly, letting the flow of animated words wash over her without interruption.

The trauma of the past weeks had taken their toll of her nerves. How she had longed for this day! Yet it had ended in anti-climax. Sure enough, she had been acquitted, but only for lack of proof and evidence. In the eyes of the world she was still the negligent nurse who had killed a famous pop star by giving him an overdose of morphine.

She would never forget the crowd outside the court. Faced with their jeering and hostility, she had felt quite ill. At that moment, more than at any other, she had needed Alec and the support of his love. But there had been only John Gorton with a kind word in her ear and a firm hand on her arm.

Why had Alec not been there? She had told the lawyer that he was required at the hospital. Only to herself could she admit her bitterness at the fact that her fiancé had not found a way of being with her when she had needed him so desperately.

'Well?'

As if in a daze, she heard Marcella's question. With an effort Roumayne jerked herself back to her surroundings. Engrossed in her thoughts, she had taken in almost nothing of what the girl had been saying. Only a few phrases had penetrated her consciousness. Art school. ... Paris. ... Eugène. ... A disjointed garble of meaningless words.

Now Marcella had stopped talking. She was looking at Roumayne in a way which indicated that she was waiting for an answer. 'Well?' she asked again. Her whole expression was one of breathless expectancy.

Roumayne stared back at her helplessly. 'What is it you want?' she asked at length.

'Will you do it?' There was a light in the blue eyes which to Roumayne, the nurse, was a sign of over-excitement.

'Will I do what?'

The pretty mouth curved petulantly, and the expectancy was replaced by impatience. 'Will you take my place at Rusvlei?'

'Take your place?' A frown appeared between Roumayne's eyebrows.

'Jeepers!' Marcella slammed the cup on to the table with a gesture of exasperation. 'You haven't heard a word I said, have you?'

'Not enough to make sense of it,' Roumayne admitted ruefully.

'Okay, I'll tell it to you again. Only this time, do me a favour and listen.' She curved her lips in a beguiling smile. 'Look, honey, I want you to pretend to be me for a few months.'

'Why?' For the first time Roumayne felt a spark of interest.

'I've been summoned home, and I don't want to go—not yet anyway. You and I could be twins. You could take my place. Nobody would ever know.'

'I couldn't do that,' Roumayne protested.

'Of course you could. It would be ideal for us both.' There was a hint of slyness in the wide blue eyes. 'You've become quite a notorious celebrity in the past few weeks. I bet you'd be glad to get away from all the publicity.'

Roumayne studied Marcella silently for a long moment. Surface appearance was all they had in common, she realised. In an odd way she could not help admiring the other girl's audacious self-confidence. It must help her in situations where Roumayne's own shyness created a disadvantage.

Common sense told her to dismiss Marcella's suggestion out of hand, yet she could not help being curious.

'Where is your home?' she asked.

'In the Eastern Transvaal.'

'A farm?'

'Citrus.' Marcella grimaced. 'Morgen upon morgen of oranges and lemons and grapefruit.'

Where nobody would know me. The tempting thought flashed through Roumayne's mind, instantly to be discarded.

'You said you'd been summoned. . . .'

'Correct.' A note of weariness crept into Marcella's tone, as if she resented going over the details of her story again. 'I've been in Paris for just over two years—art school. I had the most divine time. For a while now my grandparents have been asking me to come back, but I managed to stay on. Now . . . the summons has come.'

'Is there a reason for it?'

'Yes.' A sigh. 'Apparently Eugène Hugo, the man I'm supposed to marry, is showing signs of impatience.'

'And you expect me to take your place as his wife?' Roumayne was incredulous.

'That *would* be complicating things.' Marcella giggled. 'No. But I want you to go there and get yourself engaged to him. I'll be back before the wedding.'

'Aren't you engaged, then?'

'Yes, of course. But not officially.'

'Why don't you go back yourself now?'

'I'm not ready to.'

'Why not?' Roumayne could not help being amused. Marcella's childlike audacity had its own brand of charm. Perhaps it appealed to this man Eugène Hugo.

Marcella rolled her eyes dramatically. 'I've met

the most gorgeous Frenchman. He came back with me from Paris. He wants me to spend some time with him.'

'Are you in love with him?'

'Madly!' Blue eyes shone with such radiance that Marcella looked suddenly beautiful.

'Then,' Roumayne shook her head in bewilderment, 'why do you want to marry the other man? Eugène Hugo?'

'Because he's rich and I'll be mistress of Hibiscus Vale.'

'Perhaps you don't really love the Frenchman,' Roumayne suggested, shocked by the girl's mercenary calculation.

'I adore him. But I wouldn't marry André. He's an artist, and struggling at that. I just want to have a last marvellous fling before I settle down to domesticity with the oh-so-respectable Eugène.'

'I understand,' Roumayne said slowly.

'I knew you would!' Marcella clapped her hands in excitement. 'Now we can just get down to discussing the details.'

'I said I understand.' There was amusement in Roumayne's tone. 'That's not the same as agreeing to your request.'

'But you *must*!' Excitement vanished, to be replaced by a childlike sulkiness.

'No.' Roumayne's voice was firm. 'I'll be getting married myself soon. I'm sorry, Marcella, but I just couldn't do something like this.'

For the next few minutes charm vied with petulance as Marcella did all she could to change Roumayne's mind. At length she took a scrap of paper from her bag and scribbled a few words. 'Take my address,' she said, getting to her feet. 'If you change your mind you'll know where to get hold of me.'

Three hours had passed since Marcella had left. Roumayne had been alone all that time, and the unhappiness of the day had grown to a feeling of depression. She had gone out to buy some buns and the evening paper, but the buns were still in the packet. After she had read the front-page article, with its cynical analysis of her acquittal, Roumayne's throat had dried up so that she could not have eaten even if she had had an appetite. It was clear from the way the piece had been written that even in the eyes of the press her acquittal hinged not on the proof of her innocence but on the fact that insufficient evidence had been brought forward by the State to prove her guilt.

Everything she possessed had gone into the defence of the case: the legacy left her by her parents after their death in a motor car accident, the savings she had accumulated in the time she had worked. All was gone. And for what? she wondered now. She was free, sure enough. But the freedom held little sweetness when the world regarded her as a murderess.

Even just now, in the lift, when she had returned with her purchases, she had been aware of averted eyes and of tongues which had begun their gossip

the moment the lift doors had closed behind her.
Jackie James, the young singing idol who had en-
thralled millions with his throbbing voice and vibrant personality, was dead through a negligent
overdose of morphine. And though it could not be
proved, the facts surrounding the incident pointed
to Roumayne being the nurse who had adminis-
tered the morphine.

The doorbell rang. Alec—at last! At sight of the
beloved face with the intelligent eyes and the sensitive lips, the depression lifted. With a cry of gladness Roumayne thrust herself into his arms and
burst into tears.

She had not meant to cry. Through all the weeks
of tension and unhappiness, through the case itself,
in fact until this moment, she had managed to keep
her emotions under tight control. But now, as if a
spring was uncoiled, she could keep calm no longer.

After a second Alec's arms came around her, and
he held her while she poured out the grief and sor-
row which churned like a torrent within her. At
last the weeping lessened, and she was able to look
at him.

'I must look a wreck.' She tried to smile, but her
voice was ragged.

'You're never anything but beautiful.' Alec's
arms had dropped to his sides, and he was standing
a little away from her. 'In any event, it's understandable. You've been through a lot.'

'And all for nothing.' She took his hand and led
him to the sofa. She sat down and waited for him

to settle himself beside her.

'That's true, in a way.' He was still standing. After an indecisive moment he sat down in an armchair a little way from the sofa. Roumayne felt a pang of disappointment. Didn't he know how much she needed the comfort of his closeness?

'You've read the papers?' she asked after a moment.

'Yes.' Alec took his pipe from his pocket and began to light it. In a detached sort of way Roumayne noted that his hands were not quite steady.

'John Gorton was bothered all along by the lack of evidence,' she remarked sadly.

'I know.'

'Do you think people will ever believe in my innocence?'

'Of course.'

This time her consciousness registered the fact that his answer came a little too quickly, was a little too pat. The strained expression in his face, his awkward posture in the chair, suggested unease. Without quite knowing why, Roumayne began to tremble.

'Alec . . . darling. . . .' Nervousness made her voice unsteady. '*You* believe me, don't you? *You* know that I didn't kill Jackie James?'

'You don't have to ask me that. You know I believe you.' He sounded angry. For a moment his eyes met hers, then slid away to focus on a lamp, as if the object had assumed an all-engrossing claim on his interest.

'Something's wrong.' It was warm in the room, yet an icy chill was creeping through her veins.

'No.' Still he could not meet her gaze.

'Yes! There *is* something. I don't know what it is, but from the second you arrived you've been ill at ease.' A moment of silence. When Roumayne spoke again her voice throbbed with urgency. 'What is it, Alec? You *must* tell me. You owe it to me.'

He did not speak immediately. As if for courage, he drew on his pipe. Tensely Roumayne watched him. Even before he spoke she knew what was coming. Strange that the thought had not entered her mind before.

'I do have to tell you.' His voice was steadier now, and he turned his gaze to the small white face of his fiancée. 'There's been talk at the hospital.'

'It needn't affect us.' Her voice was small but defiant.

'Brave words, Roumayne, but not quite true. I'm just starting out. My career is not yet off the ground. . . .' He paused uncomfortably.

'I'd be in your way.' An icy numbness enveloped her, but her mind and her emotions were fully under control now. 'People would wonder about a doctor whose wife might have been a murderess.'

She waited for him to deny it, but he didn't. 'I'm afraid that's so,' he conceded unhappily.

'And that would worry you, Alec?' Her voice was tinged with contempt.

Alec's head jerked up sharply, and a red stain of embarrassment appeared on his cheeks. 'I've worked very hard to get where I am now, Roumayne.'

'Of course. I was a fool not to think of it.' By sheer effort of will she managed to keep her movements steady as she pulled the ring from her third finger of her left hand. Quietly she passed it to him.

'I feel an absolute heel.' Alec's voice was thick with embarrassment and his own movements were jerky as he put the ring into his pocket.

'You needn't.'

'We can still remain friends, Roumayne....' He looked across at her, his eyes pleading for understanding.

'No, Alec.' Her voice was very low.

'I'll always love you.' He reached for her hand, but she pulled it from him.

'Don't go on, Alec.' Inwardly she wondered that she was able to maintain this appearance of outward calm and decision. 'Let's make it a clean break.'

She got to her feet and he followed her to the door. 'Goodbye, Alec.' A tiny pause. When she continued there was a catch in her voice. 'If you ever think of me—remember the good times.'

The icy calm remained with Roumayne as she dialled the number written on the tattered scrap of paper.

'Miss Du Toit?' she asked matter-of-factly when a girl's voice answered the phone. 'Roumayne Mallory. I've change my mind. If your offer is still open I'd like to accept it.'

Half an hour later Marcella Du Toit sat in the

armchair which Alec had vacated, and expounded on the details of her plan.

'It can't fail.' Her face was alight with eager confidence.

'I hope you're right.' Roumayne's voice was low and steady as it had been in her interchange with Alec. It was only by keeping a tight rein on her thoughts that she managed to stay calm. 'You're quite certain that nobody will suspect I'm not you?'

'Not for a moment,' Marcella replied gaily. 'I've been away from home a long time, and in Paris at that. It's only natural that there'd be a few changes.' She laughed. 'And there *have* been changes. I'm not the shy innocent farm-girl who left Rusvlei two years ago.'

There was a quick brittle vivacity in the other girl's face. No wonder the gorgeous Frenchman wanted to spend some time with her, Roumayne thought drily. Marcella was not the only one who would enjoy the fling.

'You'll have to brief me fully,' she commented. 'I don't want to make an elementary mistakes. How will I know who everybody is?'

'I've thought of that.' Marcella opened her bag and drew out a pocket-sized photo album. 'I've photos here of my folks.'

Roumayne listened silently as the other girl told her about the different people featured in the album. It seemed that Marcella's parents had died when she was a child, and that she had been brought up by her grandparents. They looked old and a little frail, and Roumayne, with no relatives of her own, wondered that Marcella had the heart to deceive them.

A page was turned and Roumayne's eyes narrowed at sight of the face staring back at her. 'Somebody else I should know about?' she asked.

'Eugène Hugo.' Marcella's voice was off-hand.

Roumayne's head jerked up sharply. 'Your fiancé?'

'The same. At least,' she corrected herself, 'my fiancé-to-be.'

For a long moment Roumayne studied the photograph. Eugène Hugo was not at all the type of man she had imagined as the future husband of the gay and irreverent Marcella. Perhaps he had been unaware that the picture was being taken, for it was clearly unposed. There was a hint of hardness in the stern unsmiling face, a suggestion of strength and authority. It was a face which robbed Roumayne of the confidence that she could pull off the deception successfully.

'This man will think I'm you?' she asked at length.

'Definitely.'

'Tell me a little about him.'

'Not much to tell.' Marcella yawned. 'He's one of those dedicated farming types—unimaginative, boring, rather dour. Not at all like my darling André.'

'Yet you insist on marrying him?' Roumayne eyed her disbelievingly.

'Of course. I told you, Roumayne, he's fabulously

rich. And Hibiscus Vale is just the most divine place—as long as I don't need to spend too much time there. I'll have to talk Eugène around to letting me spend lots of holidays in Johannesburg.'

Sceptically Roumayne looked at the lean rugged-featured face. He did not look the type of man to be talked around. On the other hand, she had no doubt that Marcella knew how to use her feminine wiles to best advantage. Perhaps the marriage would turn out all right, but its success did not concern her. All that mattered was that Roumayne would have a few months in a quiet place, a chance to lick her wounds away from the public eye. Now that even Alec was lost to her, all she wanted was to spend some time in seclusion. She needed a while to regain her shattered spirits, so that eventually she could make a new life for herself. One advantage of Marcella's proposition was that Roumayne's stay at the farm would cost her nothing in rent or food. This was an important consideration now that her savings were exhausted and the hospital had indicated that she could no longer work there.

Roumayne looked up as Marcella went on speaking. 'I want you to get engaged to Eugène.' Her manner was restless. 'I can't be bothered with the bore of going through an engagement period, it's so utterly silly. I'll just get back before the wedding. Then you can quietly disappear, and I shall take my rightful place.'

'And how do you propose that I pull off the engagement?' Studying the other girl, Roumayne wondered how it was possible for two people, so similar in appearance, to have such different personalities.

'Nothing to it.' Marcella shifted impatiently in her chair. 'As I told you, it's always been taken for granted that we would marry one day.'

'Do you mean the engagement will be announced the moment I arrive in Rusvlei?'

'No. I suppose you could say it's an understanding. Eugène is just waiting for my return. I'm quite sure of that.'

'I see. . . .' Roumayne eyed Marcella thoughtfully.

'There is an incentive, Roumayne.' The pretty mouth curved slyly. 'If you pull it off, in other words if I return to a wedding, I'll see to it that you're amply rewarded.' The slyness deepened. 'Don't forget that I'll be the wife of a very rich man. You can probably do with some money?'

Roumayne hid her anger at the malice in the words. They talked a while longer. There were matters of clothes and of transport to discuss, more background details which Roumayne would be expected to know. Mercenary Marcella might be, but she was shrewd with it. She had thought out the plan well. At last she rose to go.

'Just one thing,' Roumayne said, a little curiously, as they walked to the door. 'Doesn't it worry you that I'll be living in your home?'

'Should it?' Marcella looked blank.

'I'll be staying with your grandparents.' Roumayne paused. 'It hasn't been proved that I didn't kill Jackie James.'

'For heaven's sake!' Marcella laughed gaily. 'Of course you didn't. I've never doubted your innocence.'

CHAPTER TWO

IT happened that Roumayne reached the little town of Nelspruit quite a while before she was expected. Only a few other passengers alighted from the train, and they soon left the station. Nobody took any notice of her on the near-deserted platform. It was apparent that whoever it was who would fetch her would only arrive later.

A little dispiritedly she glanced at her watch. At least an hour to wait. She was tired after the journey, and thirsty. A cup of coffee would make her feel better.

As she left her luggage at the station and made her way into the town, her spirits lifted. She had not known it would be so tropical here. Vivid shrubs grew in profusion, bougainvillaea hibiscus and poinsettia, their red and purple and orange blooms making great splashes of colour on walls and fences. Jacarandas lined the steets. These trees were now in flower, creating great clouds of misty mauve above the brighter hues of the tropical shrubs. Sparkling in the sunshine, the small Eastern Transvaal town had a charm that was irresistible.

Roumayne walked for a while, enjoying the brightness and the crisp fragrant air, then she saw a restaurant and went inside. Instinctively she chose a corner table, slightly hidden behind a tall potted plant. The recent weeks of unhappiness and notoriety had created in her a desire to be inconspicuous which was near to obsession.

The coffee was strong and hot and nerve-steadying. Despite all that Marcella had told her about her life on the farm, Roumayne could not help feeling anxious. If only she did not make any mistakes! If only nobody guessed her true identity. She would not be able to bear it if she had to leave her temporary refuge under a cloud of disgrace. Besides, she had a great wish to spend some time here. Already she could sense that a few months in this lovely part of the country would go a long way to restoring her serenity.

All at once her attention was caught by a couple at a table near the entrance of the restaurant. Perhaps she had been so engrossed in her thoughts that she had not seen them come in. The woman was beautiful. Her hair was black and glossy and coiled in a chignon at the base of her neck, thus enhancing perfect features and a flawless ivory skin. An expensive low-cut blouse revealed a voluptuous figure, and she was possessed of a poise which struck Roumayne as almost incongruous in this small country town.

But it was her companion who claimed Roumayne's greatest interest. She did not need to see him stand up to know that he was tall. He was not handsome, at least not in a conventional sense, but his tanned rugged features had a rakish look, giving him an appeal and distinction which would make him irresistible to many women, Roumayne sensed.

Certainly his companion found him irresistible. Roumayne doubted whether either of the two tasted the food they ate. They were far more interested in each other. The women was gay and vivacious and tantalising, and the man responded to her charm with unmistakable relish.

So absorbed were they in their conversation that from her table in the corner Roumayne was able to study them unobserved. It came to her that the man was familiar. Almost certainly she had seen him before. As a nurse she had met so many people over the years. The man did not have the appearance of a doctor, nor could she remember him as one of her patients.

The trial. ... There had been dozens of reporters and photographers. Had he been sent to Johannesburg to cover the trial? Blood rushed to her cheeks. This town was so small, and though the farm was apparently some way out, it would be inevitable that she would come in for an occasional shopping trip. What would she do if she were to meet him, if he recognised her, and let out her secret?

Nervously Roumayne glanced at her watch. The minutes were passing. She did not want to walk past the couple near the entrance, yet it would soon be time for her to return to the station. . . .

The man was smiling. He leaned very near to his exotic companion and said something in a low voice. The woman laughed huskily and reached out a playful hand to touch his lips. Then they were getting up from their table.

Relieved as she was to see them go, Roumayne could not help wondering where they intended to continue their very obvious mutual enjoyment.

She reached the station and reclaimed her luggage. She was just looking for a bench when someone called, 'Miss Marcella!'

Spinning round, she met the beaming grin of a face she recognised. 'Hello, Amos.' She smiled back at him in relief. 'How are you?'

'Very good. Ow, Miss Marcella, too long time that you leave here. We think you never come back.'

'And here I am.' She was still smiling as Amos took her suitcases and led the way to the car. She had learnt from Marcella that this man had grown up on the farm. At sixteen he had started work on the lands. Now, thirty years later, he was the indispensable right-hand man of the elderly Du Toits. He had watched Marcella grow up from babyhood. Yet, without question, he had accepted Roumayne in her place. Perhaps the deception would run a smoother course than she had feared.

Enchantment took the place of anxiety as the car left Nelspruit and took the road past Karino. The road cut through citrus estates. The trees, dark and lush-looking, were laden with fruit; oranges and naartjies, lemons and grapefruit. Now and then, when there was a break in the citrus, there were farms with mangoes and avocadoes. Beside the road, at regular intervals, stood tall feathered palms and the red flames of poinsettias, alternating in an exotic spectacle of colour.

And then they were turning off the main road, and anxiety returned. Roumayne's heart beat uncomfortably as the car bumped over the stony track. Without asking Amos if they had far to go, she knew that her journey was nearing its end.

Amos stopped the car to open a pair of high closed gates suspended over parallel cattle tracks, and Roumayne saw a signboard with the name 'Rusvlei' lettered in white paint, and underneath, faded almost to illegibility with the years, 'J. Du Toit'. She had thought that her anxiety had reached its peak, but when Amos started the car once more, and the farmhouse appeared in sight at the end of a jacaranda-lined drive, Roumayne's nerves caused a hard knot of pain to form in her stomach.

Hardly had the car drawn up in the shade of a spreading maroela tree when an old man appeared on the stoep and hurried down the steps.

'Marcie!' A weatherbeaten hand reached out to her as she got out of the car. 'My dearest child!'

'Oupa....' The word left the parched throat on a whisper as Roumayne bent to kiss the wrinkled cheek. 'It's ... it's so good to be here.'

She turned for her suitcases, but Oupa Du Toit pulled impatiently at her hand. 'Amos will bring your things. Ouma has been waiting for this moment.'

An old lady was waiting at the top of the red stone steps. How could you stay away so long, Marcella? Roumayne wondered, as she saw the tears of joy in Ouma Du Toit's eyes. Frail and bent like her husband, she could only walk very slowly, and Roumayne, her trained eyes always on the alert, knew that she suffered from arthritis.

Tea was waiting, and great platters of home-made food—all Marcella's favourites, Roumayne assumed. Melktert, light and delicious. Golden koeksusters, dripping with syrup. Wholemeal scones, spread with butter and konfyt.

'You made all this, Ouma?' The intimate family titles came with surprising ease after the first anxious moments, when she had wondered whether they would spot the deception.

'Can you imagine Ouma letting somebody else do it?' Oupa beamed with pride and happiness.

'No, of course not,' Roumayne said gently. 'I only thought arthritis might make baking painful.'

'You see that I have arthritis?' Ouma was clearly astonished at her granddaughter's unaccustomed perception.

'I think you mentioned it in one of your letters,' Roumayne said hastily. How could she have allowed herself to slip up so stupidly!

'I did? It's not too bad, *meisietjie*. Some days are better than others.' A slight frown deepened the creases on the wrinkled cheeks. 'You are so thin, child. Didn't they feed you in Paris?'

'We were always on the go there. There was so much to do.' Summoning a gay laugh, Roumayne tried to make little of the difference between her figure and Marcella's. It was one of the things which had worried her, the fact that Marcella's frame was a little fuller than her own.

'The child will fatten on your good food, Anna,' Oupa commented cheerfully. 'And they say the men like thin girls. Not like in our day, eh? I always enjoyed having something to squeeze.'

'*Siestog*, Jan!' But there was laughter in the reprimand.

The talk turned to Paris. The grandparents wanted to know about Marcella's life there, and the girl had given Roumayne enough background, even some anecdotes, so that she would be able to talk easily about the two years away from the farm. After a while she fetched a few of the canvasses Marcella had given her. The pictures were gay and inconsequential, conventional scenes which Roumayne had seen many times before. The Eiffel Tower, views of the Seine, a gendarme with his distinctive peaked cap. Marcella could certainly draw, for the pictures had been deftly executed. But though the grandparents enthused over them, Roumayne herself doubted that their artistic quality had justified the long absence from home.

Eventually Ouma changed the subject. The smile left her eyes as she asked, 'Will you go over to Eugène's place later on?'

'Won't Eugène visit me?' Roumayne put the question lightly, a little flippantly, as Marcella would doubtless have done.

'I don't know....' Ouma's voice was uncertain.

'He knows I'm back?' A slight nerve of apprehension quivered through Roumayne's system. Something in the old lady's manner told her that all was not quite as Marcella had told it.

'He knows, *ja*.' The two old people exchanged a troubled glance. After a moment Ouma said, 'You were very naughty, Marcie. We kept asking you to come back.'

'I was so busy in Paris....' Roumayne could not help being annoyed that she had to defend Marcella.

'Marcie, Eugène is a man. Did you expect him to wait for you for ever?'

'You're not saying Eugène is married?' A nerve throbbed in her temples. If the man was indeed married, there would be no reason for her continued presence in this lovely place. And even if she did stay till Marcella felt like returning, there would be no financial reward at the end of her stay, no money with which to begin a new life.

'He is not married,' Ouma said. 'But impatient. And....' She hesitated. 'I must tell you, Marcie, there has been talk that he has been seen with another woman.'

'Is that all?' Roumayne remembered what Marcella had had to say about Eugène. Dour, boring, a dedicated farmer. Perhaps he had been seen discussing his crops with a woman. In a simple farming district that would be enough to cause comment.

'Do not make light of it.' Oupa looked as troubled as his wife. Roumayne knew from Marcella that her grandparents had always wanted a match between the two young people so that the adjoining farms could be amalgamated. Something about a river which ran through Eugène's Hibiscus Vale. . . . Now they were clearly worried.

'I'm sorry.' She smiled her apology. 'Don't worry. Of course I'll walk over and say hello to Eugène.'

The ground was soft and mauve with the fallen flowers of the jacarandas as Roumayne walked back along the way she and Amos had driven earlier in the day. Perhaps Marcella would have chosen a different manner to visit Eugène's farm. Roumayne doubted that she would have walked. In all likelihood she would have gone by car, but for Roumayne, not yet familiar with the ways of the family and the farm, walking was preferable.

She was enjoying herself. Earlier in the day it had been scorchingly hot. Now the heat had grown less, and the jacarandas threw long shadows over the drive. Roumayne had bathed and then changed into a pretty halter-necked sun-dress, one of the dresses Marcella had given her. She would have to spend a few evenings in the privacy of her room, altering Marcella's clothes so that they would not hang on her. Temporarily, however, a few safety pins artfully hidden in strategic places made the dress look as if it had always been her own.

She had been pleased with her appearance in the mirror. Her own taste was different from Marcella's, more tailored perhaps, and more simple. Yet now that she was dressed in Marcella's clothes, and with her hair cut and shaped in the other girl's soft flowing style, their similarity was intensified. They could indeed have been twins.

Roumayne's earlier nervousness had vanished. Marcella's grandparents had been taken in by the act. There was no reason why Eugène should not believe it likewise.

The entrance to Hibiscus Vale was more imposing than that to Rusvlei. Two big white gates were flanked by tall hibiscus, the scarlet trumpet-shaped flowers flaring riotously over the gateposts. As Roumayne walked along the drive which, she assumed, must lead to the homestead, she saw plantations stretching to either side. It seemed that Eugène did not grow citrus as the Du Toits did, but that he went in for tobacco. His fields had an air of lushness, the plants looked strong and healthy and grew in rows of geometric profusion.

She came quite suddenly upon the homestead. At a bend in the drive she had her first sight of the house, and she paused for some moments to study Marcella's future home. It was very big, long and white and sprawling. Its gables were white and high and distinctive, curving in a manner that suggested Cape Dutch architecture, and over the walls wisteria climbed in a misty profusion of lavender. Like the tobacco plantations, the house had an air of luxury. Without knowing quite why, Roumayne sensed that the interior would be furnished with casual elegance and with no expense spared. She did not need to enter the house to know why Marcella wanted to be its mistress.

A servant answered her knock. After a wide smile of recognition she was told that Eugène was in one of the tobacco barns. The words were accompanied by such copious gestures that Roumayne found her way to it without difficulty.

At the entrance to the barn she paused. After the glare of the sun she had to adjust her eyes to the dimness within. She could just make out the shape of a man bending over a piece of machinery. He must be the man she sought.

'Eugène?' She tried to inject into her voice a gay confidence she did not feel.

She saw him straighten and turn her way. After a moment he put down the tool he was holding, and came to her.

'Long time no see,' she began, still in the same inconsequential tone. 'Did you know that I . . . .'

The words died on her lips, and a quiver of recognition shivered through her system as he stopped before her. He was the man she had watched in the restaurant, the man who had flirted so enjoyably with the exotic brunette.

For a long moment neither of them spoke. His hands were stuck negligently into the waistband of his jeans, and his eyes studied her with an indifference that was almost insulting. If he was glad to see her, he was certainly not letting her know it.

'So,' he said at length, and his tone was as neutral as if he had been addressing any one of his acquaintances. 'You're back, Marcella.'

'Yes.'

With the tip of her tongue she moistened dry lips. For no reason at all her legs felt suddenly weak. Why on earth had she not associated the man in the restaurant with the photo Marcella had shown her? She could only think it was because the trial was still uppermost in her mind, its memories still so raw that she had instinctively thought the man must be a reporter.

He was watching her. A hint of amusement touched the strong lips. 'What a very monosyllabic answer!'

'What did you expect me to say?'

She stared at him as if mesmerised. He had changed from the more formal clothes he had worn in the restaurant. The T-shirt he wore now hugged the contours of his body, revealing broad shoulders and a muscular chest tapering to narrow hips. His working jeans moulded long taut thighs. His throat was strong and muscular, and as tanned as the arms and the rugged-featured face. There emanated from him a suggestion of power and strength and authority, and a hint of latent ruthlessness which gave Roumayne a moment of fear.

She tried to remember the photo Marcella had shown her. Dimly she recalled the impressions which had come through to her even then. But Marcella's description had done a lot to dispel the impression.

Boring and unimaginative, she had called him, a far cry from the gorgeous André. That he was in every way different from Marcella's playboy friend, Roumayne could easily believe. But boring and unimaginative? Even without knowing him, Roumayne realised that those adjectives could not be applied to Eugène Hugo. She wondered where Marcella's eyes had been in all the years she had known him.

'I thought you'd be babbling away about Paris the moment you saw me.' His smile was lazily audacious. 'Lost your tongue, Marcella?'

'Aren't you glad to see me?' She was stung by his tone.

'Let's just say that I don't have strong feelings either way.' The comment was dry.

'You're not very lover-like,' she said recklessly.

'Only a lover can act like a lover.' The quiet tone was sardonic.

Involuntarily Roumayne remembered his zestful response to the woman in the restaurant, and she wondered how long he had been back at the farm since the rendezvous. She took a deep breath. The conversation was not following the lines she had imagined. The dull unimaginative lover, panting for Marcella's return, eager to place a ring on her finger and to make her his bride, was turning out to be a man with a self-assurance she had never before encountered.

'Shall we sit somewhere and talk?' she suggested uncertainly. She needed a few moments to think, to regain control of the situation.

'By all means. How remiss of me not to have thought of it myself. I'll be with you in a moment, Marcella.'

He went back into the barn and made a quick final adjustment to the machinery he had been working on. Then he came back to her.

'Let's go up to the house.' His voice was matter-of-fact. 'Joshua will give us something cool to drink.'

As they walked Roumayne was disturbingly aware of the man beside her. His stride, deliberately slow so that she could keep pace with him, was long and easy. He was very tall, a sideways glance told Roumayne that she would take him just to his shoulders. Alec had been the same height as she was. She was not accustomed to such tallness, nor to such an aura of almost tangible maleness and virility.

To one side of the house was a wild fig tree, very big and very ancient. Its trunk was gnarled and its branches spread welcome shade over a large area of sun-drenched lawn. The ground surrounding the tree had been paved with slasto, and held a garden table and chairs. It was here that Roumayne sat with Eugène.

Joshua, the house-servant who had earlier told her where to find Eugène, brought out a tray; a cold drink for Roumayne and a beer for Eugène, a platter of sandwiches for them both.

When he had gone back into the house, Eugène asked, 'Well, Marcella, and how *was* Paris?'

'Wonderful.' And then, remembering Marcella's manner of speech: 'I had *the* most divine time.'

'Learn anything about art?'

Roumayne looked at him sharply, but the rugged face was bland. 'Of course.' She slanted him a provocative glance in a manner that was quite foreign to her own nature. 'Wasn't that my reason for going there?'

'Was it? I never really knew.' Still the maddening neutrality in his tone. She had the uncomfortable feeling that he was laughing at her.

'Why did you think I went, Eugène?'

He really was the most disconcerting man she had ever met, but Marcella expected to see an engagement ring when she returned so it was necessary to pursue the conversation. Perhaps if she could draw him out a little she would discover more about his relationship with Marcella. But one thing she knew already—Eugène Hugo would not be anywhere as easy to get along with as the elderly Du Toits.

He was watching her with lazy amusement. 'The bright lights?' he suggested.

'Really, Eugène!' Pretending to be offended, she made her mouth stiff with dignity and disapproval. It was uncanny how well Eugène knew Marcella. 'Don't you know that I went to Paris to study art?'

'Ah, art.... Of course.' The wicked brown eyes were laughing at her. 'And when do you intend to hold your first exhibition?'

'No need to be facetious.' Involuntarily a glimmer of a smile escaped her. It occurred to her that Marcella would not have the complacent husband she expected. But that was Marcella's affair. For herself she was beginning, unexpectedly, to enjoy the interchange.

'My apologies.' There was nothing apologetic in the low mocking voice. 'Tell me, Marcella, have you come home for a visit?'

'A visit?' She stared at him, taken aback. 'I'm home for ever, Eugène.'

'Really? Forgive me, my dear, but I can't help wondering how you're going to settle down at the farm now that you've seen Paree.'

He was laughing at her again, but Roumayne heard the underlying seriousness in his tone.

'That rather depends on you.' She forced a smile beneath long spiky lashes.

'Really?' His eyebrows rose as he studied her across the small table. His pose was one of utter detachment and relaxation. Long legs stretched out before him, and a well-shaped tanned hand lifted a glass of beer to his lips. The eyes that rested on her face were lazy. 'Why so?'

'Isn't that rather a strange question for a future husband to ask?' Roumayne queried deliberately.

'You've cast me in that role?' His smile was more mocking than before.

'Well, yes, of course. . . .' Her voice quivered with sudden uncertainty.

'How very unwise of you, Marcella.' His voice was dry.

She was disconcerted. Everything had gone so well up to the point when she had set out to visit Hibiscus Vale. Why had this disturbing man stepped out of the picture Marcella had painted of him?

'Why am I unwise?' she asked at last, wishing that she could control the slight trembling of the hand that held her glass. 'After all, we are engaged.'

'No,' his voice was firm, 'we are not engaged, Marcella.'

Helplessly she looked at him. Nothing in his posture had changed. But there was an implacable hardness in his eyes, and she was once more conscious of the strength and confidence which enveloped him. Added to this was a masculine virility which made her acutely uncomfortable.

A little desperately she cast her mind back to the conversations with Marcella. The girl had been so certain of the understanding between herself and Eugène. All that was necessary to make it official was a ring on her finger. A ring which she, Roumayne, must procure if she wished to have the stability of some money when the time came for her to leave this place.

'We're not officially engaged,' she conceded, summoning a nonchalance she did not feel.

'We're not in any way engaged. Officially or unofficially.' His look was level with warning.

'But....' She paused helplessly.

'Yes?' His voice was very polite.

'There's always been an understanding. I mean, we've both known we would be married one day.' In her nervousness the words tumbled out too quickly.

'There was a time when we assumed that, granted.' It was said very quietly.

'Aren't we saying the same thing, then?' She looked at him in confusion.

'I don't think so.' Eugène drained his glass and set it down on the table. When he looked across at her his glance was steady. Let's stop sparring, Marcella. You say we were unofficially engaged. I don't agree. There was a vague understanding, but that's all it amounted to.'

'You mean ... you want to get out of it?' Although the rejection affected Marcella and not herself, Roumayne could not rid herself of the feeling that she was being jilted for the second time in two days.

'Yes—to the extent that I was ever in it.' Eugène's voice was deceptively casual.

'Why?' she asked quietly, wondering how Marcella would have handled the situation. With hysterics or with dignity?'

'Does there have to be a reason?' His eyes were narrowed.

'I think so.' She studied him for a long moment, taking in the strength of the broad shoulders, the authority and power in the lean tanned features. Could she take on a man of this calibre and hope to get the better of him? Determinedly she pushed the thought from her mind. She *had* to get the better of him. If she failed, she would have to begin life after a few months at the farm, with not a penny to show for lost time.

'Your parents always wanted a match between us,' she observed quietly, remembering the background detail Marcella had supplied so offhandedly. 'And my grandparents want it too.'

He nodded agreement, not seeking to deny what she had said.

'Then why are you backing out now?' She was intrigued despite the apparent hopelessness of the situation. How could Marcella have been so foolishly sure of her position?

Eugène was watching her, a slight smile curving the corners of the strong mobile lips. When he spoke it was not to answer her question. 'Did it ever occur to you, Marcella, that I might have questions of my own?'

'Questions?' She could feel the tension tightening in her belly. Though she had never been possessed of Marcella's brand of outrageous self-assurance, till now she had been able to cope with most situations. In the course of her work there had been fractious patients and difficult doctors, and she had learnt to deal with them. But this man, Eugène Hugo, and this particular situation, made her feel uncomfortably out of her depth.

'Certainly.' His voice was expressionless. 'You

were in no hurry to get back from Paris, Marcella. Why?'

She should, of course, have anticipated this question, and had she realised the nature of the man she would have to deal with she would have been prepared. In the circumstances she could only say, with a great show of injured dignity, 'I was studying, Eugène.'

'Not all that time, my dear.' He made no attempt to hide the taunt in his eyes. 'You were to have been back at Rusvlei months ago.'

'I decided my studies required further time.' She tried to match his detachment, and knew that she failed. Mentally she cursed Marcella for not having provided her with iron-clad excuses. And wondered at the same time if this perceptive man would not have seen through them all anyway.

'Your dedication to your vocation is touching,' he mocked her.

'And your sarcasm is totally unnecessary,' she burst out with a spurt of indignation which she hoped would do Marcella justice. 'Why the hell is it so strange that I should be devoted to my art?'

He studied her for a long moment without speaking, his gaze outrageously sweeping the wide blue eyes, the tawny hair, the tightened angry lips, then descending to the slender curves of her body.

'What would you say,' he drawled at length, 'if I told you that I never believed in the artistic purpose of your visit to Paris? My impression of you, Marcella, is that of a butterfly.' He grinned wickedly at her bemused expression. 'A beautiful butterfly, to be sure. But frivolous and restless and aching to spread its wings in a gayer place than Rusvlei.'

He was right, of course. It came to Roumayne with a flash of insight that this man would almost always be correct in his assessment of people and situations. Just as he would always be in control. Of all the men she had met in her life, and unhappily she had to include Alec, she had never come across a man who possessed the strength and vibrant sense of confidence of Eugène Hugo. It occurred to her also that this man could never be the right husband for Marcella. Such were his arrogance and self-assurance that he would always have to be the dominant partner in a marriage, and this was something that wilful fun-loving girl would not be able to tolerate. But all these thoughts were neither here nor there. She had set out to achieve something, and she had to find a way of doing it.

'People can change, Eugène,' she said quietly. 'Perhaps I *was* the butterfly you thought me. But two years is a long time. Can't you understand that I could have changed?'

Tensely she waited for his reply, for upon that depended not only whether he would concede that he and Marcella were engaged, but also whether he would accept any essential differences which must inevitably exist between Marcella and herself.

'I do understand that.' It was said without mockery this time. 'You have changed, Marcella, I saw that immediately. But, my dear,' he paused a moment, as if to lend greater emphasis to the rest of the sentence—'I've changed too.'

Her throat was dry with apprehension, and the amethyst eyes were wide as she waited for him to continue.

'You talk of an understanding, of the fact that our families always thought we would marry.' He leaned back in his chair, crossing his long muscled legs. 'What does all that mean in this day and age, Marcella? We've gone beyond the time of match-makers, when marriages were arranged according to the whims of families. As for there being an understanding ...' he snapped his fingers impatiently, 'there was never a formal engagement. Just a vague assumption that we would marry one day because, for a variety of reasons, it seemed the natural thing to do.'

'And that assumption no longer holds good?' she watched him curiously. Despite the hopelessness of the situation, she was intrigued by this man with the lean tanned face, the mouth that was strong yet mobile, the eyes that could change in a flash from mockery to amusement to seriousness.

'Neither for me nor for you.' An eyebrow lifted sardonically. 'You won't deny that if you're honest, Marcella. You made your own indifference to me quite clear by the way you kept prolonging your absence. When you did return it was only in response to a virtual command from your grand-parents.'

Was there anything this man did not perceive?

For a frightened moment she wondered if he could see through the deception. But no, on that score it seemed she need not worry. He had noted the change in her personality, but was content to put it down to the long absence in a bustling metropolitan city.

He raised a long-fingered brown hand to glance at his watch. 'I don't like to sound rude, but I have an appointment in half an hour, Marcella.'

With the sophisticated brunette? An unexpected pang shot through Roumayne's nerve-stream at the thought. She put it down to the fact that the beautiful woman was a further complication towards the achievement of her aim.

'I must be off myself, Eugène.'

They stood up at the same time, and once more she was aware of his towering height.

'I'll walk with you to the stables,' Eugène offered.

'The stables?' She looked at him uncomprehendingly.

'Didn't you have White Star taken there?'

'Oh!' She could not hide the flush that spread over her cheeks. She had made another slip. Had he noticed it? Brightly she said, 'I walked.'

'You did?' The brown eyes were curious as he looked down at her. 'And I believed you wouldn't be able to wait to get on to White Star's back.'

'I felt like a walk.' The defiance in her tone was not entirely forced. 'I've had so much of streets and pavements. I wanted the feel of good clean earth beneath my feet.'

'You really have changed, Marcella.'

He was smiling. For once there was no trace of mockery, and she was struck by the warmth that lit the brown eyes, and the laughter which deepened the crevices about his mouth.

They were a little way down the drive when the idea came to her, and she wondered why she had not thought of it before.

'I could make you change your mind about an engagement,' she said in a voice that was low, and, she hoped, seductive.

'Really?' Again the amusement was in his eyes. Also a spark of interest.

Beneath spiky black lashes Roumayne slanted him her most provocative glance, the kind of glance she imagined Marcella bestowing on the gorgeous André. She made her voice low and throbbing. 'Like this?'

Boldly she took a step towards the tall stranger and leaned toward him. She found she had to stand on her toes in order to get her lips to his. His lips were cool and unresponsive, and his arms remained at his sides, but she could not accept the rebuff. Her arms came up and twined themselves about his neck, one hand burying itself in the thick black hair at the base of his head. And all the while she wondered at the depths of helplessness which could produce such daring.

She felt him stiffen, then grow rigid. Then two hands gripped her shoulders and he put her a little way away from him. He cupped her chin in his hand, forcing her to look at him. An unreadable expression was in the brown eyes which stared intently down into blue ones.

After a moment she saw his mouth descending. His arms pulled her close and she readied herself for his kiss. No longer were his lips unresponsive, but neither were they tender. With a pressure that was relentless his mouth pressed down on hers, forcing her lips apart till his tongue touched her teeth. The arms around her became two bands of steel, tightening about her, drawing her even closer, moulding soft curves against taut muscled lines.

His response shocked her, numbing her senses, her thoughts, the memory that her initial overture had been no more than part of a calculated act. The touch of his lips, his tongue, the muscled thighs pressing against hers, awoke an ardour she had never before experienced. She forgot that she was acting the part of Marcella as her senses took over and she twined herself even tighter against him.

With an abruptness that was shocking, he pushed her away from him. For a moment the sense of abandonment was such that she felt ill. Her knees were weak; she felt drained, and at the same time filled with an excitement that was well-nigh unbearable.

She looked up at him. He was very pale, and his breathing was ragged, as if her ardour had unnerved him almost as much as it had unnerved her. But he regained his composure quickly. His eyes were narrow and inscrutable as he met her gaze.

'Well?' She was breathless. 'Have I changed your mind?'

He laughed, a laugh that was wicked and low. 'Let's just say that you've given me something to think about.'

'I haven't proved that we're suited?' She was incredulous that he could remain unconvinced after what had just happened between them.

'You've proved that you're a lot more experienced than when you left here.' His voice was seductive yet mocking. 'You must have had some good tutors.'

The dart found its target. 'As if you're so lily-white and pure!' she burst out resentfully. 'I....' In time she stopped herself from using the word 'saw'. 'I hear that you've been keeping pretty sophisticated company.'

'Yvette Stacy *is* sophisticated.' His eyes mocked her as he confirmed the accusation.

Then he looked once more at his watch. 'Sorry to cut short this intriguing encounter, Marcella, but I'm late.' Eugène grinned, white teeth flashing in a tanned face. 'Be seeing you, my dear.'

CHAPTER THREE

Two days passed quietly and without incident. They were days in which Roumayne did not see Eugène. He did not visit her, nor did she feel it appropriate to take the road to Hibiscus Vale again so soon. It would seem too much like running after him, and hardly the best way to get a ring on her finger.

She did not regret the respite. Slowly she was settling into the routine of Rusvlei, and after her first period of anxiety, in which she feared every moment that she would do something wrong and be discovered, she began to enjoy life at the farm. Casting her mind back over the past years, she could not remember a time when she had been so at peace. When she was a nurse in a busy hospital, every moment had been programmed. To this had been added the trauma of the trial and its consequences.

Though she knew that she had had nothing to do with the death of Jackie James, it had never occurred to her that the world would not accept her version of what had happened that night. The final straw had been Alec's faithlessness. Strange that she had never anticipated it. She had always known Alec to be ambitious, but she had never dreamed that he would abandon her when she needed him most.

In the quiet moments of the night, pain twisted at her chest when she thought of Alec and of the way in which their life together had ended before it had ever begun. It was only when the tears stopped flowing that practicality took over and showed her the good side. Better that Alec should have revealed the weakness in his nature now, before they were married, than later, when it would have been too late. And yet, despite all logic and reasoning, the pain remained.

It was a pain which might conceivably lessen at Rusvlei. Already she knew the farm to be a haven. Life moved slowly, healthily, adapting itself to the changing seasons and the demands of the crops. The people here were kind and affectionate. True, their attitude towards her stemmed from the fact that they believed her to be the real Marcella, but despite this knowledge, their affection was a healing balm to Roumayne's shattered nerves.

More than ever, now that she had learned to know the elderly Du Toits, Roumayne found it difficult to understand that Marcella could have left them for so long. The two old people seemed to live for the girl, wanting to know every detail of her life in Paris. Often Roumayne found herself having to improvise, and her inventive though perhaps inaccurate replies seemed acceptable to the grandparents.

As much as she could, Roumayne tried to adopt some of Marcella's personality, her exuberance, her quickness of speech. But it is one of the most difficult things in the world to act out of character for any length of time. The strain of attempting to be what she was not proved so great that, gradually, Roumayne let more and more of her own personality take over. It was only to be expected that two years would have wrought their changes. Ouma and Oupa Du Toit were enchanted with her gentleness, her sweetness, her willingness and ability to ease difficulties caused by rheumatism and arthritis.

The one fly in an otherwise smooth ointment was Eugène Hugo. Sooner or later she would have to meet him again. And if she wanted to leave Rusvlei with enough money to begin a new life, she needed his ring on her finger.

It was odd how much the thought of another meeting with the man disturbed her. It was a disturbance that was out of all proportion to what she must, in the circumstances, regard as a job. It was a job which had seemed relatively uncomplicated when Eugène had been no more than a remote but eager bridegroom, dour and boring and dedicated to his crops. The man who had revealed himself as arrogant, masculine, forcefully virile and not at all eager to be engaged was a different proposition entirely.

The man meant nothing to her. The very nature of the circumstances made it quite impossible that he could ever mean something to her on a personal level. Why then did the memory of their encounter set the blood flowing faster in her veins?

These were her thoughts as she stood at the kitchen table baking scones. Ouma had intended to bake them herself, but Roumayne, compassionate of arthritic fingers which took on chores for love despite the accompanying pain, had gently but firmly taken over the task.

The scones were in the oven and she was putting away the last of the utensils when she became aware that someone was watching her. She spun around. A warm flush spread over her cheeks at the sight of the tall figure leaning in arrogant carelessness against the doorpost.

His legs were long and powerful in well-cut riding breeches. A polo-necked sweater hugged the strong throat, and when he moved a muscle rippled beneath the thin fabric which covered his chest. His appearance, vital and compelling and utterly male, struck a primitive chord inside Roumayne.

She swallowed nervously. 'You could have said you were here.' Here voice was defiant, and her hand moved quickly to brush a loose tendril of hair from a damp forehead.

'Why?' He drawled the word arrogantly.

'It's not polite to watch people when they don't know you're there.'

'And since when have you been so concerned with politeness, my dear Marcella?' The low voice was edged with mockery. 'Such a transformation Paris has wrought!'

'What do you mean?' Immediately she was on the defensive.

'Let me think. . . .' His mouth curved in amusement. 'Your preoccupation with good manners is new. And, since we're being so very polite, would you mind me saying that it's most unexpected?'

When she made no reply his eyebrows lifted sardonically. 'And now the question of your domesticity,' he continued, his grin edged with malice. 'I suppose your grandmother drummed it into you that the way to a man's heart is through his stomach?'

'Anything else?' she asked with deliberate stiffness, though inside herself she was amused once again at his deft assessment of Marcella's personality.

'There's your sexual expertise.' The brown eyes glinted wickedly. 'A definite step forward.'

The amusement vanished as Roumayne felt an almost uncontrollable urge to tell him what she thought of him. But for the present she had to keep the peace, so she swallowed the words.

'I take it you don't approve of the change?' Amethyst eyes beneath long thick lashes slanted a glance that was provocatively demure.

'Did I say that?' His gaze moved slowly and intimately over her body, coming to rest at last on soft lips and a heightened colour. When he spoke again his voice was seductive. 'In fact, I would say that I am pleasantly surprised.'

'I'm flattered.' Roumayne turned back to the sink so that he would not see the expression which his tone had called forth.

'And so you should be.' His voice was dry. 'I've

asked that White Star be saddled. We're going for a ride.'

At his words a flicker of fear shivered through her. Roumayne could ride, but her experience was limited. She could trot, and could manage a slow canter, but there her ability ended. Instinctively she knew that Marcella would be an accomplished horsewoman and a daring one, revelling in fast gallops and risky jumps.

Sooner or later Roumayne would have had to ride, but she would have preferred to start off on her own, practising along quiet trails through the veld.

'You've taken a lot on yourself,' she observed with a great show of iciness, and with the kind of annoyance she felt sure Marcella could evince.

'Have I?' The dark eyes were curious. 'Your third day back, and as far as I know you've not yet ridden your favourite horse.'

'I've been with the old people.' Her eyes skittered nervously away from the too-penetrating gaze.

'Your concern for your grandparents is touching.' A hand reached to the back of her neck, long fingers alighting with a sensual touch on her throat.

Roumayne felt her body grow rigid as her senses reacted to Eugène's closeness. The man was possessed of a sexual attraction that was more potent than anything she had ever encountered.

'I ... I might ride later,' she stammered.

'Now!'

The authoritative ring in his voice made it a command. A quick glance at eyes which had taken on the aspect of flint made it clear that he was not accustomed to being disobeyed.

In theory she could have protested; she was not so timid that she did not have a mind and will of her own. There had been many times in the past when she had had to stand up for her convictions in awkward situations. But there was something about this man which seemed to defy protest. More important, if she refused to agree to a request which was normal enough in the circumstances, the deception would soon be at an end.

She took a deep steadying breath. 'I adore White Star,' she said as firmly as she could. 'But ... but I don't like to be ordered around Eugène.'

He did not answer. The hand that had held her throat curved round to cup her chin, forcing her to look at him. A time-stopping moment, when she thought he would kiss her, sent the adrenalin pumping through her veins, and her senses readied themselves for the embrace.

There was no kiss, just the penetrating gaze from the lean chiselled face. By the time he released her, her heart was pounding so violently that she felt certain he must hear every beat.

'Five minutes,' he informed her crisply as he turned on his heel and left the kitchen.

It was not only in looks that Roumayne and Marcella could have been twins. Their height was also similar. Marcella's riding breeches were a trifle too big at the waist, but two safety pins made an effec-

tive alteration. As Roumayne looked at herself in
the mirror she was conscious of her quickened
breathing. The breeches and the crisp white shirt
she had chosen to wear with them emphasised the
trim curves of her figure. Her hair was brushed
sleekly back behind her ears, and only a touch of
lipstick was necessary, for her cheeks were still
flushed with pink, and her eyes were blue with a
radiance which had been missing for as long as she
could remember.

She could not deny to herself that she was pleased
with her appearance. But the reason for her pleasure was simply the knowledge that the change of
scene had already begun the healing she had hoped
for. The fact that the tall disturbing stranger would
be seeing her at her prettiest had no significance
whatsoever, she told herself firmly.

Nevertheless she could not help being acutely
aware of him a few minutes later when she found
him waiting with the horses. A lifted eyebrow ex-
pressed surprise when she did not leap into the
saddle, as was evidently Marcella's custom, but
looked at him for help.

'Out of practice?'

'I didn't ride in Paris,' she informed him breathlessly. The touch of his hands on her body as he
hoisted her on to the saddle set the blood pounding
once more in her veins. For once she was glad. Such
was the sensual effect of his nearness that she forgot
to be nervous of the horse beneath her.

'Paris seems to have done many strange things for

you.' He was laughing as he mounted his own horse, a gleaming black stallion which reflected the same proud arrogance and strength of its owner. 'Let's go!'

After the first few minutes, Roumayne knew that she could hold her own. White Star was a quick, lively horse, yet gentle with it. As she felt more at ease Roumayne began to enjoy the outing. The sky was clear and very blue. Later it would be hot, with a heat that burned down on land and man and beast, but now the air had a freshness that was like champagne.

They had left Rusvlei and were now riding through the fertile tobacco plantations of Hibiscus Vale. Once again Roumayne was struck by the lush perfection of Eugène's lands. Not that she was surprised by it. It seemed to her, even after such a brief acquaintance with the man, that anything he undertook would be accomplished with efficiency and competence.

The stallion kept always a little ahead of the smaller horse. Now and then it snorted impatiently, and Roumayne sensed that it was only the authority and superior strength of its rider which prevented the proud black horse from breaking into a gallop. Though the stallion could have been no simple beast to control, Eugène sat easily in the saddle. Horse and rider had much in common. There was the same strength and arrogance, a sense of almost overpowering virility. No wonder, Roumayne thought, that they seemed so at ease together.

They came to some tall round buildings, and here they reined in their horses. It seemed there was something Eugène needed to inspect. Without comment this time, he held out a hand to help her down. For a single moment Roumayne tingled all over with an electric-like shock that seemed to pass from his hand to hers. She caught her breath as she shot him a swift glance from beneath lowered lids. His face was devoid of expression, but the brown eyes were watchful. Roumayne wondered if he had guessed that for a moment she had been swept by an unexpected and uncontrollable wave of desire.

The buildings had to do with the tobacco, and in an attempt to regain her composure Roumayne began to talk about farming. She had never seen the crop growing, and knew nothing at all of the processes which took place between the time of harvesting and the moment when the neatly-packaged cigars and cigarettes found their way into the shops.

Yet she had to be careful. However uninterested Marcella might be in the subject, her only enthusiasm being for the wealth earned by tobacco, the girl must inevitably have picked up some knowledge about the crop.

Eugène responded to her few careful questions in greater detail than she had hoped. As he talked Roumayne's inner turmoil subsided, and she found herself growing fascinated with the whole process of tobacco farming, with its inherent problems and its lucrative potential. For once there was no mockery in Eugène's expression, no arrogance or sarcasm.

The light in his eyes stemmed from a dynamic vitality and enthusiasm.

He was a man living in a man's world, Roumayne thought, and found herself comparing him with Alec. Like Eugène, Alec had been engrossed in his work, and had been ambitious. So ambitious, she thought wryly, that when it came to making a choice between his career and his feelings for Roumayne, his career had come first.

Unless she misjudged him greatly, Eugène was ambitious in a different way. She had no doubt that he could be ruthless, but she did not believe that he would ally success with status, or that he would let himself be influenced by the judgment of others. Rather, all his endeavours would be directed to farming for its own sake. If he found ways of dealing with diseases of the crop, ways in which the quality of the tobacco could be improved, the knowledge he acquired would be shared with other farmers. With Eugène success would never be measured in terms of status. It would only be a matter of personal pride and achievement and joy in his work.

Fleetingly Roumayne wondered how she could know so much about the man in such a short time, but she did not doubt that her assessment was correct.

They were emerging from the tobacco kiln and were about to remount their horses when there came the sound of screaming. In seconds they were at the scene of the accident. A man lay on the ground, blood pouring from his face and arms. His screams were even worse than the sight of the blood. He was in obvious agony.

The role of Marcella was instantly forgotten as the nurse in Roumayne took over. The bleeding was so profuse that it took some moments to ascertain the site and extent of the wounds, then it appeared that the man had been injured by a tractor. His companions were in the grip of a panic caused by fear. Of all the men, only Eugène remained calm, though even beneath his tan was a tinge of pallor—almost unconsciously, Roumayne registered the sight. Then she forgot everything except the need to stop the bleeding, and the relief of the man's pain.

She took charge without asking permission. Matter-of-factly she directed those around her, so that each person who could be of help did what he was bidden, and the rest were crisply despatched from the scene.

An ambulance was sent for. By the time it arrived the injured man was out of danger, though still needing the kind of attention which could only be had in a hospital. Roumayne was filled with a sense of exhilaration and achievement as she watched him being lifted into the vehicle. It seemed a long time since she had done any nursing.

Roumayne was unaware that the workmen watched her with a kind of awe amounting to reverence. Nor that the tall lean man at her side was studying her with an intentness which took in every detail of her appearance; the soft swell of the breasts heaving rhythmically beneath the sweat-moistened blouse, the hair which had long since escaped its neat style and which fell in tawny tendrils across a smooth brow, and the amethyst eyes which sparkled with such radiance that a pretty face was made beautiful.

'You handled that well.'

The simple words were spoken quietly. She stared up at him. For a short while she had been in another world, the nursing world which had been hers until so recently, and for that brief space of time her awareness of her surroundings and of the people therein had faded. Now Eugène's words had jerked her back to reality.

'It was nothing.' She spoke without thinking, knowing only that what she had done was little enough compared to what had been expected of her in the past.

'I wouldn't say that.' There was unexpected warmth in the slow searching gaze.

Suddenly shy, Roumayne was unable to meet those disturbing brown eyes. Instinctively she turned her head away.

A hand reached out to cup her chin, and as he had done before that morning, he forced her to look up at him. She met his gaze as if mesmerised. The workmen, as if in tacit understanding, had vanished. Roumayne and Eugène could have been two people alone on an island where all movement, all life, hung in a limbo of suspended time.

The hand left her chin and moved backwards, to encircle the base of her throat. A thumb began a slow, sensual stroking movement, sending flickers of hot flame shivering from her throat down along her spine, and constricting her lungs so that she could hardly breathe. Memory of their first meeting came rushing back, bringing with it the feel of his arms about her body, the touch of his lips on hers. Quite suddenly she was swept by a longing to be close to him, to feel his arms around her once more as they had been then.

On that first day she had sought to prove something on behalf of Marcella. Now it was her own body which sought the same thing for itself, with an insistence that was disconcerting.

What she felt was irrational and ironic. Above all, it was dangerous. It was one thing to assume the outward appearance of Marcella. It was quite another to invest herself with the emotions which should belong to the other girl. It was particularly foolish when she knew that such emotions could only lead to heartbreak. Roumayne had come to Rusvlei to get away from unhappiness. The last thing she needed in her life was a complication which could bring further unhappiness.

With an effort she pulled away from Eugène. 'The horses will get restless.' Her voice was brittle. 'Shouldn't we ride?'

'Sure.' His tone was quite expressionless as his hand dropped to his side.

They rode a while longer through the tobacco

plantations, emerging quite suddenly in a great stretch of uncultivated land. This was pure bush-veld. The turf was hard and rough beneath the hooves of the horses, and the sky above was blue, with just a few wisps of white cloud to relieve the glare of the sun. There was evidence of recent rains. Wild flowers, orange and yellow and white, dotted the scrub, and the distant kopjes, so often dusty and brown, had touches of green. The air was fragrant with the smells of the veld, the spicy aromas of the yellow mimosas mingling with the acrid scent of the khakibos. Monkeys scampered along the branches of maroelas and knobthorns, and once a duiker appeared from behind a bush. It stood quite still, ears pointing upwards, sniffing the air. Then with a graceful bound it vanished in the long grass.

It was very still in the veld, an all-encompassing stillness that seemed to drown the sounds of the birds and the insects and even the quarrelling of the monkeys. It was quiet and peaceful. Beautiful and healing. Involuntarily Roumayne uttered a small cry of delight.

The black stallion was alongside her. The rider turned his head, his eyes smiling a question.

'It's so beautiful,' Roumayne said joyously.

'It's never been any different.' His tone was curious.

'Of course,' she said quickly, feeling suddenly ruffled with the need to explain. 'It's just ... the peacefulness hits you after the hustle and bustle of Johannesburg.'

It did not need the raised eyebrow to make her aware of her slip.

'The hustle and bustle of Paris too,' she prattled on, the words tumbling out a little too fast as she improvised. 'Especially Paris, of course. I mean, all that mad traffic, and the jabbering of the people. If you want to experience noise, go to Paris and....'

He was not to be sidetracked. 'You said Johannesburg.' His voice was soft and more dangerous for it. The smile had left his face, and his eyes were hard.

'Okay, so I was in Johannesburg too.' Roumayne tried to speak flippantly though she could not help shifting uneasily beneath the steady gaze. 'There's no plane that gets you straight from Paris to a farm in the middle of the bundu.'

His face was a study of contempt, but, as if it was beneath his dignity even to attempt to show the emptiness of her excuse, he remained silent.

'And ... and once I was there anyway. I stayed a while....'

'A long while.' It was said with implacable certainty.

'What the hell does it have to do with you if I was in Johannesburg?' Her burst of defiance was only in part an improvisation of the way Marcella might be expected to react in the same circumstances. Roumayne herself felt genuine anger at the sheer arrogance of the man.

'Absolutely nothing—as I'm not the prospective bridegroom you seem to want.' He spoke with sardonic quietness. An expression of contempt appeared in his face. 'That doesn't stop me from being curious. Tell me, Marcella, did you never think of your grandparents?'

'They allowed me to go to Paris.' She met his eyes challengingly, wishing all the time that she stood on firmer ground.

'For a year,' he agreed. 'To indulge you.' Once again it was apparent that Eugène had no high regard for Marcella's artistic talent. 'They missed you every minute of that time, yet you made every excuse to prolong your absence.'

'Because I needed to further my studies. But I've already told you that.' She tossed back the remark recklessly, and saw the strong mobile lips curve in a smile of undisguised derision.

'Your studies in what, Marcella?'

'Art, Eugène.' Roumayne injected into her tone all the dignity of which she was capable.

'I hope your progress was worth while in terms of time and money.'

'You can see my canvasses and judge for yourself,' she said sweetly, wondering at the same time whether Eugène would be as impressed with Marcella's work as her grandparents had been.

'Some time I'll do just that.' His eyes raked her insolently. 'But perhaps you will concede'—his drawl was spiked with malice—'that an interest in the opposite sex was an important part of your studies?'

You should have briefed me better, Marcella,

Roumayne mentally reproached the other girl. *Your reluctant bridegroom lacks nothing in the way of imagination.*

Aloud she said, 'I concede it.' Defiantly she met his malicious regard, and held it. 'What of it, Eugène? Did you expect me to live in complete seclusion, devoting myself only to study?'

'I wouldn't believe it if you said that you had.' A low taunting laugh. 'All I wanted to hear was the truth, Marcella. As for the Johannesburg bit—you might as well confess. There was a man there who held your interest for more than just a passing moment.'

She was about to deny it, then thought better of it. The horses had been reined to a standstill while their riders talked. The stallion shifted restlessly, muscles rippling in the glossy neck, yet obedient to the will of the man on his back. Eugène Hugo looked very much the master, not only of the powerful steed, but of every aspect of his life. Dark hair, thick and straight, fell across his forehead. His features were tanned and compelling. His eyes, those eyes which could change in mood with such rapidity, watched her now with an expression that was compounded of amusement and derision.

However hard it was to contend with the man in these circumstances, Roumayne knew it would be doubly hard if ever he were to learn the truth. It was not impossible that the story of the dead pop singer had reached this quiet part of the country, and that a picture of herself would reveal the likeness with Marcella. The last thing she wanted was to arouse Eugène's suspicions. It was apparent that his perceptiveness had kept him from regarding Marcella as an innocent maiden with pure academic interests. In that case, why deny what was fact?

If Eugène did eventually marry Marcella— strange what a stab of pain there was at that thought—then he would have to learn to cope with the capricious, flirtatious side of her nature. By admitting a previous relationship with another man Roumayne could in fact be smoothing the way for the other girl. Equally important, it would cover the slip she had made when she had mentioned Johannesburg.

The thing to do was to brazen it out in Marcella's own special way.

'I confess.' She made the statement with studied frankness, hoping she sounded as confident as Marcella would have been. 'I did have a good time in Paris, and, for a while, in Johannesburg. What of it?' She curved her lips in a pout. 'I'll be spending the rest of my life on a farm.'

'That, of course, is up to you.' He spoke evenly, his face devoid of expression.

'Is it, Eugène?' She slanted him a glance, making her eyes wide as she flirted with him. Much as she despised herself for her behaviour, now that she had accepted the role, she had to behave like Marcella.

'Entirely.' He sat easily, almost lazily on the stallion, but there was nothing lazy in the hard brown eyes. 'I've told you that before.' He paused, then prompted her: 'So there *was* a man?'

'Yes.' A dramatic sigh in Marcella's own fashion. 'A famous artist he was, and he took an interest in a simple country girl. Can you imagine what that did to my morale?'

'Don't underestimate yourself, Marcella.' His voice was dry.

Now what did he mean by that? Better not to ask, perhaps. 'It was nothing serious,' she told him. When he did not reply she forced a hesitant laugh. 'You do understand that, don't you, Eugène?'

'Meaning that you didn't go to bed with him?' His voice was light and amused.

'Eugène!' The outburst was as shocked as she could manage. It was not hard to imagine what Marcella and the gorgeous Frenchman were up to in Johannesburg. Somewhere at the back of Roumayne's mind was the thought that this man with the stern tanned features, the strong mouth and honest eyes, deserved something more in a bride than a capricious girl who wanted him only for his money.

'Such outrage doesn't become you, my dear.' A smile sketched his lips, and his eyes glinted with an expression she could not define. 'I can't tell if you're still a virgin, Marcella, but you're certainly not the innocent little girl you pretend to be. You proved that rather thoroughly a few days ago.' Malice gleamed in his eyes. 'The artist must have been an excellent teacher.'

Once more the memory of their lovemaking came to mind. The man astride the stallion was so near to her that she could see every one of the hairs that curled on the tanned arms and muscled throat. She had a crazy desire to reach out and trace a finger along the mobile lips and the rigid line of his jaw....

In time she recalled the part she must play. A part which was becoming more and more loathsome. 'What about your sophisticated lady-friend?' she queried, as acidly as she was able. 'Is she so inexperienced?'

'Yvette?' A satisfied smile curved his mouth, and his eyes lit up as if at some private memory. 'Yvette is a woman of the world.'

'Are you still seeing her?' She hoped her eyes did not reveal her pain as she asked the question. She had to ask it for Marcella, and knew that Eugène's answer was just as important for herself.

'Naturally.' His tone was matter-of-fact.

'Then ... if you can have a good time, why do you criticise me?'

'Criticise?' His eyebrows lifted. 'I don't criticise you, Marcella. Whatever you've been up to in the past, in fact what you do now, doesn't concern me. I don't even have the right to criticise.'

Roumayne bit her lip. The situation was slipping rapidly from her control. If Marcella expected to return to a wedding she had badly assessed the position. Nobody could be further from being an eager bridegroom than Eugène Hugo. You've given me quite a task, Marcella, she thought wryly, as she watched Eugène put his heels to the stallion and saw the horse move away in a gallop.

CHAPTER FOUR

THEY were riding through cultivated fields once more, and for a while Eugène and the stallion stayed ahead. Now Eugène was wholly a farmer again, inspecting fences, testing the water levels of dams, checking whether work had been done correctly.

Then they came to veld again. At a river Eugène turned and motioned to Roumayne that he intended to make a halt. She dismounted and watched the horses pick their way over the stones to bend their heads to the water.

It was almost midday. The sun shone mercilessly from a cloudless sky, the rays scorching the countryside with their fierceness. It was a heat to which Roumayne, the city girl from Johannesburg, was not accustomed. With one hand she pushed wet tendrils of hair from a damp forehead. Her shirt clung moistly to her body, moulding itself about her soft curves, revealing the rapid swelling movement of her breasts as she breathed. With relief she saw that they were near a clump of trees, and that Eugène had chosen the spot for a rest.

They sat down on the ground and leaned back

against a high smooth rock. From the pocket of his breeches Eugène pulled a flask and passed it to Roumayne. She sipped thirstily, the ice-cold water tasting better than champagne in the heat.

'No cup, I'm afraid,' he observed as she gave the flask back to him. 'Has Paris made you too fastidious to share?'

'Of course not!' Blue eyes laughed into brown ones which were beginning to seem ever more attractive.

It was Eugène's turn to drink, and as he studied her over the top of the flask she felt a sudden flutter of her heartbeats. He was drinking very slowly, his gaze moving over her face and body with a sensual intensity which set the blood racing in her veins.

Nothing was said, not a word passed between them, but there are times when eyes speak more eloquently than tongues can do. Roumayne was the first to drop her eyes. An almost unbearable inner excitement made it impossible for her to sustain the sensual gaze a moment longer.

Deliberately she turned her eyes to her surroundings, and as before she was enchanted by the appeal of the bushveld. Its beauty must grow on one, she thought, until it would be hard to make one's home anywhere else. There was the river, the water clear and rippling. There were the trees of the veld, acacias and knobthorns, maroelas and monkey-orange. In the distance were three kopjes, grouped in a strange formation, almost like people clustering together for comfort in the wilderness.

A heat-haze shimmered and danced over the rocks, and a light breeze stirred, bringing a sensation of temporary coolness. Over everything hung the sounds of the bushveld, a ceaseless hum of millions of undefined insects.

Roumayne felt herself in the grip of a tremendous exhilaration. She tried to tell herself that it was caused by the beauty all around her, by the feeling of peace and timelessness. That it could have anything at all to do with the man at her side was unthinkable. He meant nothing to her, and never could. He was just an integral part of a job she had undertaken, a job she was beginning to regret more and more.

'Dreaming?'

The low throbbing voice brought her back to reality.

'Just enjoying the scenery.'

'Paris seems to have made you appreciate your home-ground more than you used to.' He was grinning, his teeth a flash of white against his tan.

'Perhaps it has. They say absence makes the heart grow fonder.' Lightly she threw the cliché at him.

'Absence has done that?' There was an odd emphasis in his tone. Brown eyes scanned her face, lingering over her lips, and she felt her stomach tighten with tension.

After a moment he grinned again, and she relaxed a little. 'Bet you never had biltong in Paris.'

'That's a certainty.' She was able to laugh. The remark was so totally unexpected.

'Try some.'

As she took the strip of dark wind-dried meat, his fingers touched hers, long tanned fingers against soft slender ones. For a timeless moment, which might have been no more than a second, they seemed frozen together, as if in the grip of an electric shock. Tension mounted again, and Roumayne coloured deeply as she saw Eugène's glance flicker knowingly over her taut face.

'Thanks.' Only sheer effort of will enabled her to pull her fingers from his. She sucked at the biltong. 'What is this? Beef?'

'Buck—kudu, actually.' His voice was devoid of expression.

'It's delicious.'

'Good. I went hunting a few months ago. Joshua dried the meat.'

They were talking for the sake of talking. Yet Roumayne could not rid herself of the feeling that what they were really saying had nothing to do with biltong.

'You love this life, don't you?' The question was inconsequential, and she did not know what had made her ask it, except perhaps that the need to know more about the man had, for some reason, become imperative. Unwillingly she recognised that it was a need which owed nothing to the fact that she had to know him better in order to bring about the engagement with Marcella.

'I can't imagine any other kind of life.' His eyes dwelt thoughtfully on her face. After a moment he said, 'Hasn't that always been one of our differences, Marcella?'

'Perhaps it isn't any longer.' It was odd how she seemed to be speaking more for herself than for the girl she impersonated.

'I find that hard to believe.' He was laughing, though not unkindly. 'You've always hankered after the bright lights. If anything, Paris must have increased your fondness for big city life.'

'On the contrary.' She kept her eyes on the distant kopjes, unable to trust herself to his penetrating gaze. 'I'm glad I came back. Really I am.' She wavered, not certain how to continue. 'Perhaps being away has given me a new set of values.'

In her own ears the words sounded pompous.

Eugène did not answer immediately, but after a moment a hand touched her cheek, bringing her around to face him. She forced herself to meet his regard without flinching.

'You're trying so hard, Marcella.' His voice was very soft. 'Why?'

'I ... I don't understand.' The breathlessness in her tone owed less to the fact that she would have to come up with an answer to his question than to the feel of the hard fingers, like a brand, against her face.

'I think you do. All this sudden love of the land, for one thing.'

'That *is* genuine,' she protested, on surer ground for the moment, because she was telling the truth— as least as far as it affected herself.

'Isn't it just all part of wanting me to marry you?'

The intentness of his gaze did not allow her to look away. If only he would take his fingers from her cheek! The contact made her so breathless that it was difficult to think rationally.

'No,' she managed to whisper. 'I *do* love it.'

'And you *do* want to marry me.' It was a statement more than a question.

'Our folks want it, Eugène. They've always wanted it.'

'The point is, do *you* want it?' His tone was relentless, demanding an answer.

'Yes!'

She looked at him helplessly, her eyes darkening to deep amethyst with shock, as she realised that she had spoken purely for herself. As one coming out of a coma, she tried to pull herself back to rational thought. This could not be happening. It was impossible! And if it was indeed happening, then she must find a way of stopping it before it went any further. She jerked her eyes from his face.

'Marcella.'

She heard him, but did not respond. She could not let herself look at him.

'Marcella!' His voice was sharper this time, the call of her name a command.

'Yes?' Her reply was a whisper.

'Look at me.' There was authority in his tone which she could not deny. Reluctantly she moved her head, until her eyes looked into his.

'Yes?' Her voice was tremulous.

'Tell me what's wrong.' The brown eyes were searching, lingering on the pale cheeks, on the trembling lips.

'Nothing,' she said, knowing at the same time that it was foolishness to try to deceive this man. If only he would let her look away from him, move away.... His closeness, the aura of sheer male virility was so overpowering, that she felt dizzy.

'There *is* something.' He was insistent. 'Who's pressuring you into this marriage?'

'Nobody!' The denial came out too vehemently.

'Your grandparents?' A hand reached out to grasp her wrist. She tried to ignore the tingling sensation which shot up her arm, but it was difficult when his eyes, like burnished topaz in the rugged face, searched her expression for the truth.

If only he would stop this line of questioning! She did not know if she had the strength to hide the truth from him if he persisted.

'My grandparents would like it yes....' She could not keep the rising inflection of apprehension from her voice. 'But that's not the only reason.'

'You would like to be mistress of Hibiscus Vale.' The observation was quiet.

Hibiscus Vale means nothing to me. I just want to be your wife. It seemed she could not eradicate the shocking truth from her mind.

Aloud she said, 'Yes.' She shot him a defiant look. 'I suppose you despise me for that?'

'Not at all. In fact, I appreciate your honesty.' His lips curved in the beginnings of a smile. 'You always were a mercenary little animal, Marcella. I think I would be more contemptuous if you tried to protest your undying love for me.'

In what fashion would Marcella have replied to his realism? It was true that the girl could not pretend to be in love with Eugène. If she had been, no summons would have been necessary to bring her home. It was also true that Marcella was mercenary. She wanted to be mistress of Hibiscus Vale, and the wife of a wealthy man. No matter that she regarded that man with disdain.

But Eugène's obduracy was an obstacle to her plans. Getting engaged to him would be very much more difficult than Marcella had envisaged, if not impossible. Roumayne could see no way of achieving what the other girl wanted.

The tension was now a hard knot of pain. With a little jerk Roumayne freed her wrist from Eugène's grip. She needed time to think, but for that she had to be alone. Such was the potency of Eugène's masculinity that it made rational thought impossible. Deliberately she moved a little way from him and stared at the ground.

Two beetles were pushing mounds of earth before them. The beetles were black with great spots of red on the hard shining backs. The mounds were bigger than the beetles, and that part of her mind which was not engaged with thoughts of Eugène, registered an abstracted fascination with their efforts. Then something else caught her attention —a flicker of movement in the grass.

She saw it properly a moment later. A snake! A gasp of fear, then with a lightning bound she was on her feet, and trying to clamber up the rock. The rock was smooth, and she slithered backwards as her feet failed to find a hold.

'Marcella?' Eugène's exclamation was sharp with concern.

'A snake!' She pointed a shaking finger. Again she tried to climb the rock, but in vain. She would have made another attempt, but two hands caught at her waist, pulling her back.

'What are you doing?' Furiously she rounded on him.

'There's nothing to be frightened of.'

The laughter in his eyes increased her fury. 'You call a snake nothing?' she flung at him, her voice quivering.

'Not when it's a grass snake. Look, Marcella, you've scared it away. It was more frightened than you were.'

Only a grass snake. It took some seconds for the implication to register. She stared at him, dazed, feeling the trembling of her limbs.

She did not know that she would burst into tears. Certainly, she had not intended to cry. Perhaps the fright, coming on top of the emotions of the day, had made her more fragile than she had realised. She hunched forward on the ground, her hands before her eyes, and wept.

She was never quite certain what happened next. One moment she was a sobbing heap, the next a pair of strong arms had pulled her up and she was cradled against a broad chest. The sobbing eased as she felt the strength and reassurance which enveloped her.

It was only when her trembling had quietened that she became aware of different sensations. Now it was the virile maleness of the man who held her which was dominant, the almost overpowering smell of his masculinity, the feel of hard muscle and bone, the excitement of heartbeats, strong and rhythmic against her cheek.

She drew her face from his chest and looked up at him. An unreadable expression was in the brown eyes that searched her face, lingering on the moist amethyst eyes, on the tremulous lips, on the long matted lashes casting their shadows over silken cheeks. Something in his gaze quickened her breathing, and when his mouth descended to hers she was ready for it.

The kiss began lightly, a gentle touching of lips. Almost imperceptibly it hardened, forcing her lips apart. As his lips began to explore the soft flesh of her mouth, Roumayne experienced a drowning feeling she had never known with Alec.

All thought of Marcella vanished. Forgotten was the need to play a part. Now Roumayne was only herself, a woman whose dormant emotions were inflamed almost beyond endurance. Yet even now, while bodily sensations threatened to overwhelm her, some last vestige of common sense reminded her that she must save herself before it was too late.

She brought her fists up against his chest and tried to push him away. When that failed to move him, she made an attempt to twist her lips away from his.

But in vain. His arms were bands of steel about her body, a vice-like grip from which there was no escaping. Despairingly she acknowledged to herself that she did not want to escape. As she fought him, she knew she was fighting herself as much as she fought Eugène.

A hand slid beneath her blouse to the bare skin of her back, then curved round to a soft breast. The touch of his hand on that intimate part of her body knocked the breath from her lungs.

Somehow she fell backwards. He did not release her, even then, but fell with her.

Now there was only sensation, the hardness of stone and the roughness of grass, the heavy strength of the body on hers. Thighs, taut and corded with muscle, pressed against smooth slender legs. Soft curves which seemed to fit into hard angular lines as if so designed. And all the while the hard lips tasted and explored, moving from her mouth down to the throbbing pulse beside her neck, then further, downwards, to the swell of breasts revealed by the two open buttons at the top of her blouse.

With a shuddering sigh Roumayne abandoned her fight. There was a sensual expertise to Eugène's lovemaking which defied further protest. Instinctively she arched her body towards his.

He lifted his head and gazed searchingly into the

dazed, passion-glazed blue eyes. Then, very deliberately, he raised himself slightly from her and began to unbutton his shirt.

There was no mistaking his intentions. Her body was aflame, but her mind called a halt.

'No!' The word required the effort of a scream, but it came out no louder than a whisper.

Brown eyes narrowed mockingly, resting on the bruised lips which had responded to his with such ardour, on the breasts, slightly exposed, which had thrilled to his touch.

'A token resistance?' he drawled. 'It's not necessary, you know.'

'It isn't a token.' Her voice was taut with nerves, and amethyst eyes hid beneath still-matted lashes. She did not want him to see the turmoil of emotion raging inside her.

'Come on, Marcella.' Now the tone was tinged with arrogance. 'Are you going to play the game of the outraged virgin? Surely not.'

'I *am* a virgin.' Her parched throat could only manage a whisper.

'Really?' He taunted her with his disbelief, but when she allowed herself a brief glance at him she saw an expression which she could not understand.

'What do you want?' she asked at last, uncertainly.

'What any man wants.' His tone was bland. 'What do *you* want, Marcella? That's more to the point.'

She gazed at him helplessly, her breathing ragged and uneven.

'A few days ago you swore that you'd show me just why it would be worth my while to marry you.' His lips moved back to her breasts, lightly, sensually, so that she had to fight a fresh wave of desire. At her involuntary shudder there was a low vibrant chuckle, indicating that he knew just how she felt.

'Haven't I given you enough proof?' she asked a little desperately.

A malicious gleam appeared in his eyes. 'Let's just say that you've whetted my appetite.' Now his tone was frankly insolent. 'The actual goods have still to be sampled.'

Furiously she lifted a hand, but he caught it before it could reach his face. She had wanted to erase the expression of sheer male arrogance, but he had forestalled her.

'Never try that again!' His voice was tight with warning.

'Eugène ... don't you want to marry a virgin?' she questioned, in as demure a tone as she could muster.

He did not answer her directly. 'Marriage is a big step.' His eyes were enigmatic. 'Virginity is only one of several considerations, Marcella.'

So virginity was only one of several considerations. What were the others? A dowry? Further proof of sexual prowess? Perhaps an accomplishment of which she was not even aware?

These were the thoughts which careered through Roumayne's mind later that evening, as she sat at the open window of her room. Three months must be spent at Rusvlei. Three months in which she must play a role which she had agreed to on an impulse born of despair. Three months in which to bring about an engagement, a task which seemed ever more distasteful.

She was beginning to despise herself for her own part in the matter. It seemed now that there was something immoral in trying to force a commitment upon a person when the surrounding circumstances were seeped in untruth. At the time when she had agreed to Marcella's plan she had been so filled with bitterness that this aspect of the matter had not occurred to her. There had been no suggestion that persuasion would be needed, for the Eugène of Marcella's description had been an eager, impatient bridegroom. The only deception would have been the fact that Roumayne would have worn his ring until Marcella had been ready for it. As for the question of financial reward, it had not seemed out of place that she would receive payment for what was, in its own way, a service.

Now, in the serenity of Rusvlei, in her knowledge of Eugène—ruthless he might be, but she sensed also that he would be possessed of an unshakable integrity—the whole thing seemed very wrong.

The worst of it was that there seemed no way she could get out of it. She had agreed to Marcella's

scheme, and must go on with it. The question was
—how?

When Marcella had outlined the plan in Johannesburg, it had sounded relatively simple. Now,
faced with the reality of the situation, it was anything but simple. True, neither the grandparents
nor Eugène questioned her identity. But after only
two encounters with Eugène, Roumayne realised
that he would do nothing that he did not want to
do. He was not the man of Marcella's description.
Definitely he was not a man who would allow himself to be forced into a situation against his will.

Three months. In one sense the period was too
short. It would take very much longer than that to
convince Eugène that he should consent to an engagement. In another sense the period seemed like
eternity. Three months in the company of Eugène
Hugo was not to be endured.

Restless all at once, Roumayne slipped a cardigan
over her shoulders and left the house. To one side
of the farmhouse was Ouma's garden where she
grew flowers and shrubs. During the day the garden
was beautiful, but at night it was a tropical wonderland.

The sky was cloudless and glimmered with a million stars. To a girl from a big city, where smog and
street light dimmed all but the brightest stars, the
brilliance of the heavens was spectacular. There
were gardenias in the garden, and jasmine and frangipani, and the combination of their perfumes was
so heady as to be overpowering.

It was very quiet in the garden. The stillness of the bushveld night was broken only by the never-ceasing hum of the crickets, their back legs rubbing together in the shrill throbbing sound which is the song of Africa at night.

The tropical potency stirred Roumayne's emotions, filling her with a sense of poignancy and sadness. Inevitably her thoughts turned to Eugène. But the drift of her thinking had changed. No longer was she thinking of ways in which to snare him for Marcella. Her thoughts had become purely sensory, memories of the two encounters which had left her so shaken.

As if he was with her now, she could feel the relentless lips parting hers, the hands that could grip with the power of steel, yet which could thrill a girl with the subtle sensualness of their touch. She could feel the tautness of the hard thighs, the strength of the broad chest. With the sensory memories came a sensation that was at once dizzying and exhilarating.

Why this man should stir her so intensely was something she did not understand, for she knew that she did not like him. It was impossible to have an affection for a person so filled with arrogance and brute strength. And yet, as Roumayne walked in the perfumed darkness, she had to acknowledge that Eugène Hugo had an undeniable attraction. It was a physical attraction, a sensual quality, animal-like and earthy. It was this quality which had struck her the first time she had seen him in the restaurant with Yvette Stacy.

It was one thing to recognise sex-appeal, quite another to be exposed to its power. Until she had experienced it, she would never have believed that she could be stirred so intensely, or that her senses could be inflamed to the point where they took precedence over her mind. A warm flush spread over her cheeks as recollection of her desire flooded back. In those moments when her back had been against the rocky ground, when hard lips had staked sensual possession, and the length of his torso had been moulded against hers, her body had ached with the wish to be possessed by him fully.

She had even, for a moment, wished that she could be his wife. And that was really crazy—madness. Never before had she realised that physical attraction could affect one with such devastating force. For all that, physical attraction could not be the basis for a marriage. Certainly it did not constitute love.

If she were to meet a man whom she could love, he would have to have the same qualities of intelligence and gentleness and sensitivity which Alec had possessed. Those were the qualities which she had loved in him; the ruthless ambition had only touched her life later. She told herself now that she could never be drawn to a man whose attraction was only based on brute strength and sensualness. A caveman, a Eugène Hugo.

In every way that counted Eugène was different from Alec, the man she had loved and with whom she had wanted to share her life.

Since the day of their last meeting she had deliberately put all thought of Alec from her mind. At first this had required some effort. Now, she was relieved to note, the effort had become almost negligible.

It came to her with a slight sense of surprise that it needed some concentration to bring a picture of Alec into her mind, but after a few moments she saw again the sensitive mouth, the intelligent eyes, the healing hands of a capable doctor. Alec was not for her, yet he was the kind of man she was drawn to. Perhaps when the time at Rusvlei was over she would meet a man similar to Alec. Was it too much to hope that she could love again?

Until then she would have to endure meetings with Eugène Hugo. She could only hope that the weeks would pass quickly.

CHAPTER FIVE

THOUGH it was late when Roumayne finally returned to her room and went to bed, she was awake early next morning. Gripped with a sense of unexplainable eagerness, she bathed and dressed, then made her way to the kitchen.

Despite the earliness of the hour, the kitchen was already alive with activity. Oupa Du Toit was dressed and ready to go outside to instruct the farm-workers. Ouma, giving no inch to arthritis, was frying eggs and bacon.

Filled with immediate remorse at the sight of the frail woman standing so gallantly at the stove, Roumayne apologised for her lateness. But when she would have taken the old lady's place at the stove she was pushed aside.

'Sit, *meisietjie*.' A smile deepened the wrinkles of the weather-worn face. 'Eat with Oupa.'

'I could make the breakfast,' Roumayne protested.

'I know that. But there is no need. In a day or two perhaps.' Roumayne saw the expression of gladness as the two old people glanced at each other. It was a silent interchange of joy that their granddaughter had acquired domesticity and consideration. Not for the first time she felt a pang of guilt at the deception.

'We want you to rest, to get some meat on your bones.' Oupa's voice was as gentle as his wife's. 'Come, *meisie-kind*, eat.'

'I shall get really fat.' Roumayne was smiling too as she sat down at the table, and spread a piece of warm toast with watermelon konfyt.

'Not fat, *meisietjie*. Just enough flesh for a man to know that you are a woman.'

Roumayne laughed, the sound echoing against the walls of the stone-floored kitchen. In this place she would regain her spirits, she thought, as she looked about her. The simple rustic atmosphere of the farm had a quality that was healing. The farmhouse kitchen was big, too big perhaps for Ouma's arthritic legs. The floor was stone, the walls of rough brick. The stove was old-fashioned and enormous, deriving its heat not from electricity but from coal. Gleaming copper pots stood on a shelf, partly for adornment but mainly for use. The air was filled with healthy country aromas; the piquancy of onions, the sweetness of apples, the mouthwatering smell of eggs and bacon and freshly-ground coffee.

Roumayne recalled the kitchen in the flat in Hillbrow, small and white-tiled and antiseptic, utterly impersonal. How different was this kitchen at Rusvlei, and how appealing. From nowhere came the wish that one like it could be hers.

A picture entered her mind. She saw herself standing at a huge farmhouse stove, preparing a dish of sizzling sosaties. Children bustled about the room, smiling, bright-eyed children. All at once a man entered the kitchen. He was tall and ruggedly good-looking. Of course, there must be a husband in the picture....

She let herself enjoy the dream a few moments, unaware that she was smiling. With a sense of shock it came to her that the face of the man was that of Eugène Hugo. How on earth had the person she disliked so intensely insinuated himself into her picture? It could only be because she had had so much contact with him lately. Angrily she banished him from her mind. At the same time the day-dream lost substance, becoming little more than a shadow.

She had no time to ponder the significance of the dream, for Oupa was speaking.

'Did you have a good time with Eugène yesterday?' he asked.

'It was all right,' she responded lightly, and saw the quick glance that passed between the two old people.

'You will see him today?' Ouma could not hide the eagerness in her eyes as she turned from the stove.

'I don't know.' Her breathing quickened involuntarily, and Roumayne felt a warm flush stain her cheeks.

The emotion, totally unexpected, was not lost on the old man who sat opposite her at the table. The eyes that watched her were kind yet alert.

'Eugène has said something, Marcie?'

'He's talked of many things.' Another attempt at lightness.

'You know what Oupa means, *meisietjie*.' Ouma's voice was reproachful as she brought the pan to the table and lifted eggs and bacon on to each plate. 'When will you get married?'

'I . . . I don't know that we will get married at all.' The amethyst eyes were troubled. The old couple wanted this marriage for Marcella. Roumayne was so fond of them that she would have given much to make them happy. Yet what, in fact, was there to tell them?

'What seems to be the matter?' Subtlety had van-

question. It was a difficult question to answer. On Marcella's part, of course, nothing had changed. She wanted, was in fact determined, to marry Eugène. So if Roumayne spoke solely for Marcella the answer would be simple.

But what Marcella wanted was of relative unimportance, for Eugène had stated his own reluctance in no uncertain terms. There would be no marriage unless something happened to change Eugène's mind. And it was as well that the grandparents were prepared for the disappointment.

Apart from her doubt that Eugène would have a change of heart, Roumayne no longer believed that he and Marcella were right for each other. In a way she had doubted it all along. But she knew now that Eugène would never do for the flighty, mercurial Marcella, who saw only the glamour of her status as the wealthy mistress of a big estate, while much of her time would actually be spent tasting the pleasures of Johannesburg's night-spots, hundreds of miles away. That her husband would not indulge her whims would never cross her mind. Inevitably however, she would have to understand that the life she planned could not be, and when that happened there would be friction. Roumayne saw Marcella, in her own flighty way, as being quite as strong-willed as Eugène. Neither one would be prepared to bend, to make concessions in what amounted to an entire life-style.

There was yet another reason why Roumayne found it hard to be enthusiastic about the marriage.

With an unhappy flash of revelation she understood that the reason lay deep inside herself. Not in her mind, where logic ruled, but in another part of her being entirely. Which was absurd!

'*Have* you changed your mind, Marcie?' Ouma repeated the question.

The grandparents were watching her tensely. The slight sharpness in Ouma's tone told Roumayne that she had delayed her answer a little too long. And still she did not know what to say.

'I think I need time,' she replied at length, hating herself for the ambiguity of the words.

'Time for what?' Oupa's tone was taut. His eyes were narrowed, as if he was seeing his beloved granddaughter in an entirely new light. 'Time to remember that you are a girl of the land? That this is where you belong? To remember that your home is here and not in the city?'

His words were so near the truth, where Marcella was concerned, that Roumayne winced.

'Not that,' she said quietly. 'I know where my home is.'

'What, then?'

'Just to get to know Eugène again.' She hesitated. When she continued her tone was more deliberate than she had intended. 'We may find the old affection is still there.' Why had it been impossible to use the word 'love'? 'On the other hand, we ... we may find we're not right for each other.'

A long silence greeted her words. Outside one of the dogs barked quite suddenly. Roumayne jerked in her seat at the sound. She had not realised that she was so tense.

Oupa was the one to break the silence. He spoke bitterly. 'I'd like to break the necks of those Frenchmen!'

'Jan....' Ouma tried to still him. 'Jan, it may be as Marcie says.'

'Ugh! She's had her head turned by too much glamour.'

'Maybe.' Ouma's eyes were on Roumayne, her gaze gentle yet penetrating. 'Is there something you haven't told us, *meisietjie*? Is there someone ... someone else?'

'No.' Again the untruth. Yet in the sense that Marcella did not intend to marry the gorgeous André the answer was true.

'No,' Roumayne repeated. Then, in a bid to turn the spotlight from herself: 'What about Eugène? He hasn't exactly been sitting around waiting for me. I have strong competition. The woman he's been seeing is very beautiful.'

'If you care for her type of looks.' The bitterness had left Oupa's tone, and now there was only distress, indicating to Roumayne that he was more worried about Eugène's attachment than he would admit. 'Mrs Stacy is not the right woman for Eugène.'

'Mrs?' queried Roumayne with a curiosity which she knew was not only on Marcella's behalf. 'Is Mrs Stacy a widow?'

'A divorcee.'

It was said with such unhappiness that Roumayne had a flash of insight into the situation.

'She divorced her husband to marry Eugène?' There was a sudden breathlessness which she could not stifle.

'It is what some people say.' Ouma spoke with difficulty.

'Do you believe it?' Intently Roumayne waited for the old lady to reply.

'Not the way it is told.' Firmness had returned to Ouma's tone, and Roumayne caught a brief glimpse of the woman she had once been—strong-minded, energetic, humorous, an asset to her farmer husband.

'In what way, then?'

'Perhaps Eugene paid her attention. If he did, can you blame him? He is a man. He is thirty-four, and,' Ouma paused for emphasis, 'he has had no other female company for too long.' Her tone hardened. 'Yet I do not believe that Eugène encouraged Mrs Stacy to divorce her husband. It is not a thing he would do.'

What Eugène would or would not do was debatable. But at least, having been exposed to the full brunt of his powerful sex-appeal, Roumayne could, in part, understand why Yvette Stacy was attracted to him. In addition to his physical appeal, Eugène was an extremely rich man.

'Whatever the truth of the matter,' Roumayne said, and wondered why her voice was so brittle, 'the fact is that Yvette Stacy is a beautiful woman.

She may not appeal to you, Oupa, but to the average man she must be quite a catch. At least you should be able to understand why Eugène is in no hurry to marry me.'

And then, before the conversation could become even more involved, she changed the subject. 'Breakfast was wonderful, Ouma. They never made konfyt like this in Paris. Rest a while, and I shall wash the dishes.'

The rest of the day passed uneventfully. The morning was spent in and around the farmhouse. When the household chores were done and Roumayne had been to the chicken-run to feed the fowls, she returned to the house.

In the kitchen was a basket of peaches which Ouma wanted to bottle, so that there would be a plentiful supply of the fruit during the winter months. Roumayne carried the basket to the stoep and began to peel away the furred velvety skins. The sun was high in a cloudless blue sky, and on the lands, in the citrus groves and the tobacco plantations, it would be burning hot. Yet Roumayne did not feel the heat, for the stone-floored stoep which surrounded the house was wide, and the roof hung far over it to give cooling shade.

Now and then Roumayne stopped working and with her hands lying still in her lap she gazed beyond the garden to the citrus groves, and beyond them to the distant russet-coloured hills. The view was a study in silence and peacefulness. The only sounds to be heard were those of the countryside; the occasional barking of a dog, birds calling in the great wild fig trees that gave shade to the garden; the ceaseless hum of insects in the grass.

Not a soul was in sight, yet she knew that in the orchards the farm-workers would be busy. And some way to the west, a tall lithe figure would be striding through his tobacco plantations, shrewd brown eyes inspecting his crops, or perhaps he would be astride the black stallion, riding to the furthest reaches of his estate.

At thought of that man Roumayne's heart beat a little faster. Angered by her reaction, she pushed Eugène Hugo from her mind, and went back to peeling the lush golden fruit.

Yet try as she would, there were times during the day when she could not help thinking of him. Could it be that her mind turned to Eugène only to spare her the pain of thinking of Alec? For pain there was when she remembered the cruel break-up of their engagement, the shock of Alec's faithlessness. But the pain was growing less. In fact, there were long hours when she hardly thought of Alec.

If only she did not need to focus on Eugène instead. The man was too disturbing for comfort. His physical attraction was such that just the memory of his body against hers was enough to make her breathless. It was an attraction which she had to acknowledge, though it went against the grain to do so. It was an attraction which was so powerful that it had a quality which was well-nigh tangible. Yet it was an attraction which existed purely in the physical sense. In all other ways, the ways that really counted, Eugène Hugo was not the man who could make a lasting impression on her. In fact, were it not necessary for her purposes, she would not waste a moment with him.

So she told herself. Yet as sunset neared, bringing with it a possible visit by Eugène, Roumayne was aglow with anticipation. Which was absurd! Was it possible that she could look forward so intensely to the appearance of a person she did not even like? The reason must be that Eugène was the only person for miles around who was even remotely near to her own age, and she needed companionship.

She walked through the garden to a rise from where she had an unbroken view to the horizon, and watched the sun go down. The sky was a blaze of glory over the distant hills. Scarlet and vermilion and streaks of vivid gold. In Africa there is no lingering dusk. The glory of the sunset was as brief as it was spectacular. Minutes after the sun had vanished below the horizon it grew dark. A chilling wind swept the veld, and Roumayne knew that if Eugène had intended taking her for a walk or a ride he would have been at Rusvlei long ago.

The garden and the view seemed to have lost some of their charm, and as Roumayne made her way back to the house she had an odd feeling of deflation.

There was no sign of Eugène that evening, nor the next day. Had her interest in the man been purely for herself, Roumayne would have been content to let the matter ride, believing that any girl worth her femininity did not run after a man. But her stay at Rusvlei had a purpose. Much as she revelled in the peaceful atmosphere of the farm, she must not delude herself that she was here for a holiday. Marcella had made it quite clear what she expected, and loathsome as the task had now become, Roumayne had agreed to undertake it.

The following afternoon, when there was still no sign of Eugène, Roumayne decided to take a walk to Hibiscus Vale. She stifled her instinctive reluctance, telling herself that if she were the real Marcella she would have no qualms. The two families had been neighbours long before Marcella's birth. What could be more natural than that the girl should pay a spontaneous visit?

Taking more than usual care with her appearance, Roumayne tried on various garments, only to discard them again. At last she settled for a blue cotton skirt, belted to reveal a tiny waist, then chose a matching blouse, which enhanced the colour of her eyes, to wear with it.

A critical appraisal in front of the mirror told her that she had not looked so pretty for a long while. Already the time spent at Rusvlei had worked wonders. The restfulness of her surroundings, coupled with her complete anonymity, had melted the tension from her eyes. The many hours out of doors had coloured her face and arms a pale golden honey, and had given her cheeks a soft pink-ness which was becoming. At the hospital she had kept her hair brushed back in a style that was neat but a little severe. Now it fell to her shoulders in a shining tawny mane.

As she walked down the drive to the road, with the petals of the jacarandas soft and slippery beneath her feet, she was frowning, wondering what she could say to Eugène. Her brow cleared as it came to her that she was Marcella, and that the girl would not rehearse a speech. If Marcella dropped in for a visit it would be because that was what the impulse of the moment had prompted. Any conversation with Eugène would have to be spontaneous. Above all, she must remember not to make any apologies for her visit.

As before, Joshua opened the door. He was surprised to see her. Had she not known that Eugène was away? he asked. In reply to her question he shook his head; no, he did not know where Eugène had gone, nor when he would be back.

Walking back to Rusvlei, Roumayne was conscious of the same feeling of let-down which she had experienced two days earlier, when dusk had given way to evening, and she had known that Eugène would not come. He must have left Hibiscus Vale the day after they had ridden together. Besides the fact that he had made love to her in a manner which still made her breathless whenever she thought of it, they had also talked of many things. Surely it would have been natural enough to mention that he was going away.

Why had he not told her? The answer was simple, Roumayne thought bitterly. The thought had not crossed his mind. All she meant to him was a body to be used for enjoyment. It did not occur to Eugène that she was a being with a mind, with emotions, a person who could be hurt by what appeared to be an almost deliberate slight.

She would not think about him, Roumayne resolved as she walked into the kitchen at Rusvlei. The man was not worth it. But her resolution came to nothing as she was struck by a new thought. Yvette Stacy! Had Mrs Stacy gone with Eugène?

As if to torment herself, she fetched the telephone directory and looked up Yvette's listing. There it was in black and white—name, address and telephone number. Angrily she pushed the book from her. It made no difference whatever whether or not the woman was with Eugène. Let them have joy of each other!

Yet the seed had been planted. . . . Hating herself, she went to the telephone and dialled the number. A maid answered. Mrs Stacy was away; she would not be back for a few days.

Slowly Roumayne replaced the receiver. She felt drained and empty. So Eugène and Yvette had in fact gone away together. Unbearable pictures flashed through her mind. She tried to obliterate them, but others took their place. She went outside and fed the chickens, but even the wild squawking in the fowl-run and the sight of two newly-hatched chicks failed to distract her.

What were they doing together, Eugène and the beautiful woman with the provocatively flirtatious manner? Try as she would, Roumayne could not push them from her mind, and her imaginings caused her anguish.

It was only much later that night, when she lay sleepless, that it came to Roumayne that she was treating the whole matter of Eugène's absence on a personal level. Her hours of brooding had been over the slight to herself, Roumayne, not once had she thought of it as a slight to Marcella.

She left her bed and went to the open window. Confused and unhappy, she stared out into the darkness. What was happening to her that should make it more and more difficult to remember that she was only playing a role? She was not Marcella; she was Roumayne. She had been hired, quite cold-bloodedly, to perform a task. All that was required of her was that she go about achieving her purpose with the same cold-blooded scheming with which it had been master-minded. On Marcella's return, Roumayne would disappear from the farm, and nobody would miss her. Nobody would ever know that a girl called Roumayne Mallory had lived in their midst.

Detachment was what was called for, she told herself strictly. Emotion did not come into it. As a nurse, Roumayne had had to train herself not to become emotionally involved with her patients. Kind and compassionate she had been always, but personal involvement with each person's suffering would not only have broken her spirit, it would have interfered with her efficiency as a nurse.

Why now, presented with a task of an entirely different nature, was it proving so difficult to keep her emotions detached?

It was almost as if a spell had been cast over her, so that she could no longer think of herself as playing a part. Not that she believed herself to be Marcella. Rather, it was as if Marcella had ceased to exist, and that Roumayne was the girl on whom the grandparents doted, the girl who had been made love to by Eugène, and who was anxious about his marriage plans.

Her breath was coming quickly as she realised that she was getting to the heart of the problem. For some reason, in Eugène's presence, it was becoming almost impossible to remember that she was only playing a part. It was she, Roumayne, who had felt Eugène's caresses on her body. It was she who had suffered torment at the slight inflicted by his unmentioned absence. Which was ridiculous in the extreme.

Logic told her that any slight, whether intentional or otherwise, was directed not at her, but at Marcella. And yet, strangely, logic seemed to have little to do with it. What had become of the thoughtful rational aspect of her character? she asked herself despairingly. Had she let fantasy get the better of her?

Somewhere, buried deep inside her, was a reason for what was happening, but it was a reason which she dared not let herself consider. If Eugène Hugo had cast a spell on her, then she must fight it. He meant nothing to her. The very nature of the circumstances forbade that he ever could mean something. In a short time she would leave this place which had been, in a sense, a haven. When she left it would be with the knowledge that she would never see Eugène again. It was futile to try to deny to herself that she was deeply attracted to him, but her feelings rested on a purely physical level. When she left Rusvlei the temporary madness he had induced in her would vanish of its own accord. So she reassured herself.

Slightly comforted, she went back to bed. But she slept restlessly. On a conscious level she could try to control her thoughts. The vulnerability of sleep allowed her to dream of a lithe tanned man astride a powerful horse, stooping to pluck her from the ground to ride away with her into the sunset.

CHAPTER SIX

THEY were having an early supper when Eugène walked in. He stood quietly in the doorway, a tall bronzed giant of a man, broad shoulders tapering to a narrow waist, and long legs taut and muscled in well-cut trousers. Brown eyes gleamed with amusement, taking in every detail of Roumayne's discomfort; her flustered expression, the hand that lifted to smooth back loose tendrils of hair from her forehead.

Perhaps it was the suddenness of his appearance which accounted for the fluttering sensation in her breast, Roumayne thought. There was something so disturbingly compelling about the man, a sense of maleness and virility which brought back with shocking clarity the moments she had spent in his arms, and the weakness of desire which had swept her body. A desire which even now was taking hold of her once more.

By sheer effort of will she dragged her eyes from his face, and back to her plate. It was very important that he should not guess at her inner turmoil. She forced herself to take a mouthful of food, but the sosaties which moments ago had been so delicious now tasted like paper.

Unlike Roumayne, the grandparents were quite at ease. 'Eugène,' Ouma Du Toit said, her wrinkled face creasing in a welcoming smile, 'it is good to see you. Take a chair and eat with us.'

'It's kind of you to ask.' When he addressed the old lady his tone lacked its usual arrogance. Involuntarily Roumayne looked up, wondering if he would accept the invitation. 'I would like to—if Marcella doesn't mind.'

'Why should I mind?' Roumayne's reply was a defensive question.

'You haven't had the courtesy to say hello,' he murmured as he sat down at the table.

'And you didn't have the courtesy to mention that you were going away.' The words were out before she could stop them. She bit her lips and felt warmth stain her cheeks.

The mocking gaze deepened, but Eugène made no effort to defend the accusation as he took the plate of sosaties and rice which Ouma held out to him.

'Did you go to Petersburg?' Oupa asked, mentioning the name of a town about two hours distant.

'Further than that.' Eugène's tone was noncommittal.

Oupa was not a man who travelled further than he had to. Cities did not interest him. He changed his line of questioning. 'You went on business?'

'Farm business?' Again the disturbing gaze raked Roumayne's face, lingering on the troubled amethyst eyes, resting on the tremulous lips. Despite herself, she held her breath as she waited for his answer.

'Not at all,' Eugène said. 'I didn't go on farm business.'

'Why did you go, then?' Now Oupa was frankly curious, ignoring Ouma's frowning warning to refrain from further questions.

'Personal reasons.' The friendly tone saved the words from being insulting.

'Did you go alone?' Roumayne had not known she was going to ask it. The moment the words were out she had a wish to vanish into the air. At the same time she knew that Eugène's reply was important to her.

Lazy brown eyes flicked her face and a slight smile sketched his lips. 'No,' he said, after a pause which was just long enough to be deliberate, 'I was not alone.'

Blue eyes hid beneath spiky lashes as Roumayne played with the food on her plate. So Yvette Stacy had in fact gone with Eugène. The pictures she had conjured up in her mind had not been fanciful. What did it matter? It could be nothing to her, Roumayne, with whom Eugène chose to associate. That was a problem Marcella herself would have to cope with one day.

Yet from nowhere came the recollection of the scene in the restaurant, when Eugène and Yvette had displayed such an ardent interest in each other, and in the region of Roumayne's chest was a dull pain that could not be shrugged away.

Silence had fallen with Eugène's bombshell. Even Oupa knew better than to question him further. For a while the clatter of knives and forks was the only sound in the kitchen.

At length, as if to break the tension, Ouma asked, 'You like the sosaties, Eugène?'

'Delicious.' He smiled appreciatively, and strong white teeth pulled at the skewer on which chunks of lamb alternated with pieces of green pepper and potato.

'Marcie made it.' There was a hint of slyness in Ouma's tone.

'She did?' Roumayne did not trust Eugène's

smile of interest.

'Marcie is a wonderful cook.' Ouma ignored the reproach in Roumayne's eyes. Surely she could not believe that the old-fashioned ploy would influence Eugène. It was far too obvious.

'You should just see the things she makes.' Oupa took up his wife's cue. 'Babotie, pumpkin pies. As for her cakes'—he smacked his lips good-humouredly—'light as a butterfly's touch!'

'I don't remember that you enjoyed cooking before you left here.' Roumayne knew that Eugène's friendly smile was deceptive.

'I've lived in Paris,' she reminded him. 'Parisian cooking is among the best in the world.'

'And they taught you good old-fashioned South African cooking in Paris?' A hint of laughter. Roumayne realised too late that Eugène was too perceptive a man not to have registered the slip.

'Of course not.' She made her voice stiff and dignified. 'But if you knew a little about the culinary arts you would understand that a good basic foundation helps you with all other cooking.'

'Ah!' Now he really was laughing at her.

'Marcie learned much in Paris,' Oupa put in hastily, as if in a bid to halt the reciprocal sarcasm.

'So I have already observed.' The tone was bland, but Roumayne did not miss the double meaning. Her muscles tensed as she lowered her eyes. The man was insufferable in his arrogance. 'Tell me, Marcella, you've learned so many different—arts.' He paused to allow full emphasis on the last word.

'Did you learn anything about painting?'

'Of course.' She slanted him a challenging look. 'It was the purpose of my stay in Paris.' How many more times would he ask her the same question?

'You should see Marcie's work, Eugène.' Ouma glowed with pride. 'Let her show it to you after supper.'

'Thank you.' He inclined his head graciously. 'I'd like to see it, but not tonight.'

'You are going back to Hibiscus Vale right away?' Oupa was disappointed.

'No. But it's a fine evening, I thought Marcella might like to join me for a walk.'

Lifting her head quickly, Roumayne met the speculative gaze. Her heartbeats increased as her pulses raced. Just the thought of being alone with Eugène in the darkness was enough to set her tingling with excitement.

It was a feeling she must try to fight. Even if, in the end, she lost the battle.

Woodenly, she said, 'Thank you, Eugène, but I must help Ouma with the dishes.'

'There's no need for that, Marcie.' Ouma's tone was quiet, but the look she sent Roumayne was one of subtle encouragement. 'Amos will help me.'

'So there is no obstacle after all. Unless, of course, you want to find one.' White teeth gleamed briefly in a wicked smile.

'You're quite absurd.' A little desperately Roumayne looked from one face to another. They were all three watching her, the grandparents with hope and encouragement, Eugène with an enigmatic expression in the narrowed brown eyes.

'All right, then.' She spoke with forced cheerfulness. 'It *is* a nice night to be outside. I'd have gone for a walk later on anyway.' And she hoped the words had put him in his place.

As they took a path that led away from the farmhouse, Roumayne was totally aware of the tall lithe man who walked beside her with the easy stride of a wild beast. She did not need to turn her head to look at him. Every inch of the powerful muscular body was imprinted in her mind, and her senses reeled with the impact of the sensual male virility which enveloped him. He made no effort to take her hand, but he was so close to her that now and then their arms touched, sending flames of excitement chasing along her veins.

A crescent moon hung in the sky, illuminating the countryside with a silvery radiance, and as always the perfume of the tropical flowers was heightened in the cool night air. From a distant kraal came the sound of drums, the primitive rhythmic pounding adding further and unbearable poignancy to Roumayne's maddened senses.

Desperately she wished that she had control over her reactions. Eugène Hugo meant nothing to her. He had made it clear that she meant nothing to him either. At least ... Marcella meant nothing. Strange, how it was becoming more and more difficult to remember her separate role.

Even if Eugène's feelings were to undergo a

change, the resulting benefits could only be for Marcella. Roumayne would leave Rusvlei and Marcella would take her rightful place. Perhaps Eugène would notice a difference. He was too perceptive a man not to be aware of the change. But Marcella's mercurial personality made sudden changes feasible.

Eugène would never know that Roumayne had been part of his life for a short time, that he had kissed her and caressed her and stirred her to a response she had never known. That was as it must be. She realised that. If only acceptance of the fact did not hurt as much as it did.

'You're very quiet.' His voice startled her out of her thoughts.

'What would you like to talk about?' She tried to sound flippant.

'Nothing in particular.' He seemed amused. 'It's just that it's unlike you to be so uncommunicative, Marcella.'

'How about you, Eugène?' All at once her suppressed anger surged to the fore. 'Why didn't you tell me about your trip?'

'I don't owe it to you to tell you my doings,' he drawled evenly.

'Particularly when they concern Yvette Stacy!'

Was she mad? Had she really spoken those words?

A low laugh sounded in the darkness, taunting and sensual. 'Are you jealous, Marcella?'

'Of course not!' It was said with a burst of defiance. And then, because she could not resist it:

'She *was* with you?'

'As a matter of fact, yes.' Eugène grasped her shoulder, bring her round to face him. 'Does it worry you?' he asked softly.

When she did not answer he cupped her chin with his hand, forcing her head up, compelling her to look at him. His face was a chiselled mask in the moonlight, his eyes unreadable. A wave of uncontrollable excitement swept Roumayne. She could not have dropped her eyes if she had tried.

'Does it worry you?' Eugène asked again, his tone demanding an answer.

'I don't like the thought of my future husband gallivanting with another female.' Roumayne was glad that she could sound defiant. At least that way he could not guess at the emotions which churned inside her.

'I am not your future husband, Marcella. I thought I'd made that clear.' Even in the dark she saw that his eyes were steel.

'My grandparents. . . .' she faltered.

'Very nice people, and I'm extremely fond of them. But they can't force me to marry their granddaughter.'

Pity that granddaughter was not present to hear the words for herself!

'Will you marry Yvette Stacy?' Roumayne asked it uncertainly.

There was a long moment of silence while Eugène stared down at her. She saw the tightening of his jaw. Then he relaxed, and the mobile lips curved in a smile. As she waited for him to speak Roumayne knew, with a flash of insight, that his reply was of as much importance to her as it was to Marcella. Perhaps more.

'I might.' He spoke very quietly.

'She's not your type, Eugène.' Conviction hid the tremor in Roumayne's voice.

'What do you know of my type?'

The grip on her chin tightened, and she was drawn closer towards him. His other hand went to her throat, skimming the smooth skin, descending to the base of her neck, where a pulse throbbed with unnatural rapidity, then, leaving that spot, it slipped beneath her dress to touch a bare shoulder. As the hand moved on her body, sending shock waves through her system, Roumayne had to battle to hold rational thought.

A tongue went out to moisten dry lips. She managed to whisper through a parched throat. 'She's not right for you.'

'And you think you're more right for me?' His voice was mocking.

She could only nod.

'I wonder. But you told me you'd prove it, Marcella. Shall we have another sample of proof?'

She had no chance to draw away from him, and as his arm tightened about her and his lips moved upwards from the base of her throat, slowly, sensually, she had no wish to. There was only the desire to be closer. . . .

Kisses danced over her face, light, yet seductively

tantalising. At length his mouth settled on hers, and the lightness vanished as her lips parted beneath his.

For a while that could not be measured in time, there was only sensation—the hard weight of his body crushing her to him, the hands that caressed her, igniting flames of excitement that threatened to consume her. The lips that moved over her face with an expertise that was demanding and relentless, gentle and teasing, by turns, the tautness of legs pressed hard against hers.

At some point he must have opened the buttons of his shirt, so that when he pushed up her blouse and pulled her back to him, the touch of the bare muscled chest sent a ripple of excitement through soft breasts. Her arms went around his neck, and every nerve cried for his total possession.

Lifting her in his arms, he put her down on the ground, then lowered his body on to hers. Perhaps it was the feel of the cool earth against her bare skin which shocked her back to a vestige of rational awareness. She could not give in to him. If she did she would be lost—in more ways than one.

It required every bit of her strength to twist her mouth from his. 'No!' It was a desperate cry.

Eugène lifted himself slightly away from her. It was too dark to see his expression. 'Why not?' he rasped.

'I don't want to.' The lie came out tremulously.

'Of course you do.' His laughter was harsh and unamused.

'No!' Perhaps because she had to fight herself as well as Eugène, the word came out with double vehemence.

'Don't lie, Marcella.'

'I'm not lying,' she whispered, fighting back her tears.

'You are, my dear. Tell me, do you only lie to me, or do you also lie to yourself?'

A finger touched the rapid pulse in her throat, travelled with deliberate seductive lightness downwards to her breasts. She could not control her trembling at this new onslaught of sensuality.

Eugène chuckled softly. 'You see, Marcella? You want it every bit as much as I do.'

It was hard to deny, when with every fibre of her being she ached for the hard male body to dominate hers. All she could do was to lie rigid, still, hoping that the waves of desire would recede.

'Why are you fighting me, Marcella?' He was deceptively bland.

'You know the answer.' Her voice vibrated with tension.

'You want to be a virgin on your wedding day?'

'Yes.' It was only partly the truth. She could not let Eugène possess her. If she did, the pain of the parting when it was time for her to leave Rusvlei would be even worse. She could no longer deny to herself that it would be painful never to see Eugène again.

His laughter was a taunt. 'You set out to prove something.'

'Haven't I proved it?' She asked it a little desperately.

'In the way of a slightly immature girl, perhaps.' The mockery was still in his voice. 'A full-blooded woman does things differently.'

'A full-blooded woman like Yvette Stacy?' she flung at him raggedly.

'Precisely.' The one word was spoken with quiet satisfaction.

Roumayne lay still a few seconds, while the nausea provoked by his implication washed over her. The ground was rough and cool beneath her, and the air buzzed with the song of the crickets, Eugène had sat up. Roumayne felt a sense of bereftness, her body missing the contact with his.

'Eugène,' she asked at length. 'There's something I don't understand. When you marry, don't you want your bride to be a virgin?'

He laughed softly, making her feel very young, very vulnerable. 'You asked me the same question last time we met. Do you really think virginity is the only yardstick of desirability, Marcella? I think you should understand, my dear, that when I marry, my bride will be a woman who satisfies me in every way.'

'And I don't?' She was aware, even as she asked it, that the question had nothing to do with Marcella.

'You've implied it.'

Her cheeks burnt in the darkness as she realised that this conversation in the secret bushveld night was the most daring, the most shameless, she had ever had. Certainly she was far deeper in a provocative situation than she had ever envisaged when she had given Marcella her undertaking.

Eugène laughed again, but this time the sound was soft and low and seductive in the stillness. All right, so he found her amusing, Roumayne thought with sudden bitterness. Perhaps he would be more impressed with the real Marcella. It was highly improbable that that girl was still a virgin, and her personality, together with whatever veneer of sophistication she had acquired in Paris, might just possibly give Eugène the degree of piquancy he seemed to require in a woman.

'Have I offended you?' Eugène asked.

'In a way,' Roumayne replied stiffly. 'No woman likes to think herself undesirable.'

'You really are intent on proving your desirability, aren't you?' His tone was amused.

She had no time to think of an answer as six feet and four inches of hard male virility crushed down on her once more, enveloping her nostrils with a potent masculine smell, rendering her weak with desire as hands and lips and tongue caressed and teased, bringing her seething emotions to a new crescendo. All thought vanished, drowned by the desire to be part of this vibrant man, the wish to prolong the moments of almost unbearable closeness for as long as she could.

He chose that moment to put her away from him, sitting up with an abruptness which left her feeling immeasurably hurt.

'What's wrong?' she managed to whisper.

'Nothing.' There was a hint of anger in his tone.

'Then...?'

'You're not ready for this.' His voice was remote. 'Pull down your blouse, Marcella.'

The impact of the order was like a cruel blow. Roumayne stared at him helplessly, assailed by a trembling she could not control. By his rejection he had hurt her more thoroughly than if he had struck her physically.

He was buttoning his shirt, all his movements calm and unhurried, his slightly heightened breathing the only indication that his own emotions had been involved in any way.

All at once Roumayne could bear his remoteness not a moment longer. In a flash she was on her feet and running from him in the darkness. She stopped only when she stumbled over a root and fell. Winded, she lay still. It was only gradually that it came to her that in her haste she had left some buttons of her blouse undone, and that tears were falling on her cheeks.

She wondered whether Eugène would follow her, but when there was no sound of footsteps she knew he had decided to let her make her own way home.

The magic had vanished from the scented night. She felt miserable and alone. She began to cry, properly now, letting out all the hurt and frustration and pent-up tension of the past hour. At length she got to her feet. She buttoned her blouse, her fingers clumsy where Eugène's had been so sure. In a vain attempt to tidy her appearance she ran her fingers through tangled hair. There was nothing she could do about the matted lashes and the tear stains on her face.

She could only hope that the grandparents had gone to bed, and that she would not have to meet them. Slowly, unhappily, she made her way back to the farmhouse. Luck was with her for once. But for a light in her room, the house was dark.

Sleep did not come for many hours, as Roumayne lay in bed with her thoughts. The scent of the flowers wafted through the open window and the beating of the drums still sounded in the night. It was a combination which was not conducive to rational thought. More than ever before Roumayne needed to think. Deliberately she closed the window and went back to her bed.

She had sought tonight to prove something to Eugène. In that she had not succeeded. Instead, there were things she had proved to herself. It was useless to go on closing her eyes to what was fact, to try to pretend that the fact did not exist. She must face reality or lose for ever her last chance of making a life for herself.

She was in love with Eugène. She had known it for some time now although, in an effort at self-delusion, she had tried to convince herself that what she felt for the tall tanned farmer was nothing more than physical attraction. She knew now why it had been so simple to get over Alec's faithlessness. What she had taken to be love had been nothing more than infatuation and affection. Great affection, to be sure, but nothing as devastating as the emotion she now felt for Eugène.

She had only to close her eyes for a picture of Eugène to enter her mind, with all the strength and power and sheer maleness that made him stand above all other men she had ever known. She could see the bronzed muscular torso, the ruggedly handsome features. She could feel the touch of his hands on her body, the strong relentless lips parting hers. And, as if he was actually in the room with her, she was swept with a wave of desire that made her dizzy.

She could not allow the situation to continue. There was no future in it. When Marcella's fling with gorgeous André ended, Roumayne would have to leave the farm, and she would be even more unhappy than when she had come here. Sadly she thought of Rusvlei. How enchanted she had been with its peace and beauty! It had been the haven she had sought, a refuge where she was able to recover from the trauma of the trial. And yet she had done wrong in coming here.

Shock and intense unhappiness had led her to make a decision on bitter impulse. Now she acknowledged that whatever the circumstances, she had been wrong to agree to the impersonation. What would be the feelings of Marcella's grandparents if they were to learn of it? What would be Eugène's reaction, in the unlikely event of his marrying Marcella, when he discovered that the girl he had wed was not the girl he had courted? Eugène was not the man of Marcella's description. Any man would be angry on learning the truth. But it occurred to Roumayne that Eugène's anger would be a truly terrible thing.

As it was, Marcella had laid her plans well, and the chances of the deception being discovered were remote. So both Roumayne's considerations were hypothetical. What was of far greater import was the one thing she had never even imagined.

Never once had it occurred to her that she would fall in love with Marcella's dull and uninteresting farmer. She had agreed to come to Rusvlei because it had appeared a refuge from the frightening hostility of those who wrongly believed that she had killed Jackie James, and from the shock of her broken engagement.

But the unhappiness she had had to contend with in Johannesburg would be nothing compared to what she would have to endure if she remained in the company of the man she loved and who could never, under any circumstances, be hers. Now that she had allowed herself to admit the truth, she knew that she could not continue the deception. The cost to her mental well-being was too high.

How could she bear to go on seeing the man she loved, to let him kiss and caress her, when she knew there was no possibility that they might share a future?

There was another consideration, more personal

and more selfish. At twenty-two Roumayne was still young enough to have a life ahead of her, a home, children. Was it too much to hope, she wondered bleakly, that despite all that had happened she could marry one day? Because she had fallen crazily in love with a man who was beyond her reach, did that mean that she must spend the remainder of her life alone? Surely not. Perhaps she would never love again as she loved now, but was it possible that she would meet another man some time and be sufficiently attracted to him to ensure a chance at happiness?

The possibility existed, she told herself firmly, but there would be no chance of future happiness if she did not stop seeing Eugène as soon as possible, before he could spoil her for all other men. Unhappily she realised that already, now she had known and loved Eugène, any man to whom she could be attracted would have to be remarkable.

It was one thing to know she must leave Rusvlei, quite another to achieve it. She could not just vanish from the farm. Apart from the anguish she would give to the grandparents, she owed it to Marcella not to expose her. What the other girl had planned was dishonest, but it was a dishonesty with which Roumayne had fallen in line. In the circumstances she was obliged to show the girl loyalty. It was too late to sit in judgment on Marcella's integrity.

The solution came to her suddenly, and it was so simple that she marvelled that she had not thought of it before. She would write to Marcella, asking her to return to Rusvlei immediately. Marcella had given her an address. She would write the letter in the morning.

With a solution at hand, Roumayne could sleep. But as she closed her aching eyes she knew that it was a solution which gave her no joy.

CHAPTER SEVEN

SITTING on the stoep the next morning, Roumayne wrote the letter. She gave Marcella no complicated explanations, but just told her that she could no longer remain at Rusvlei, and asked her to make arrangements to come back as soon as she could.

When she had closed the envelope she dropped it on to her lap and gazed into the distance. She had not yet decided where she would go when she left Rusvlei. Johannesburg was out—her memories of that city were still too raw for comfort. Durban perhaps, or Cape Town. Cape Town was a beautiful city and nobody there knew her. The first months would be hard, especially until she found a job. The money Marcella had promised her would have been a useful standby. But she could not wait for financial reward. The price was too high.

How she would miss the mystic beauty of the bush-veld, the unhurried calm of the farm and the surrounding countryside. The sun was high in the sky, but it was pleasantly cool on the wide shaded stoep. Here was the same sense of peacefulness as everywhere else on the farm. The cane chairs were old, but bright cushions made them comfortable. A pile of farming magazines lay on a cane table, and the red stone floor had wet patches where Ouma had watered her beloved pot-plants. In many ways Rusvlei had a casual shabbiness not found at Eugène's Hibiscus Vale. Yet for all that it had a charm which Roumayne doubted she would find again.

Hungrily Roumayne gazed at the farm-lands, wishing that she could imprint the view in her mind. It would be something for her to remember when she felt cooped-up and low. The tops of the distant mountains were still shrouded in mist, but the lower slopes were clearly visible. Here and there were patches of grey rock, but mostly they were wooded. She had looked forward to walking through those forests some day. Now that was not to be.

Nearer at hand were the farm-lands, the citrus groves of Rusvlei, the tobacco plantations of Hibiscus Vale. There was a sudden commotion as the dogs burst out of a clump of long grass, chasing a troop of monkeys. Shrieking violently, the grey vervet monkeys darted towards the nearest tree. Swinging from the branches, they made cheeky faces at the dogs barking in helpless frustration.

Roumayne watched the scene, smiling. There was an abundance of wild life in the bush. The monkeys, the occasional klipspringer or duiker, shy and graceful. Birds of all colours. Even now, on the lawn beyond the stoep, some jays, their feathers a vivid kingfisher-blue, squabbled loudly over a few crumbs. All this she would miss.

So absorbed was Roumayne in the scene below her that she did not hear the sound of a horse's hooves. Not until she heard a familiar voice ask, 'Penny for them?' did she know that she was not alone.

Startled, she spun round, her heart thudding in her chest. He looked very tall, very strong, as he stood watching her from the top of the steps. He was wearing riding breeches which showed off the striking figure to perfection. Black hair fell across a wide forehead, and there was a hint of steel in the dark brown eyes. Roumayne wondered how long he had been watching her.

'I ... I wasn't thinking about anything in particular,' she stammered woodenly, pulling her gaze back to the mountains with some effort. She did not want to look at Eugène. The sight of the rugged features affected her senses too disturbingly.

'We're going riding,' he told her.

'I'm not,' she protested, a little too quickly, her voice shaking at the thought of being alone with Eugène again.

'Yes, you are,' he informed her, not unkindly, yet in a tone that did not permit opposition. 'White Star is being saddled. Go and get changed.'

'You take a lot for granted,' Roumayne said icily.

She remembered the first time he had ordered her to ride with him. How frightened she had been! Then her fear had been of a horse, now it was of a man.

'Do I?' he drawled.

His eyes moved over her, registering the slight tremor of her lips, the rapid pulse at the base of her throat, and she knew that he remembered as vividly as she did the abandoned lovemaking of the previous night. It was one thing that he remembered her ardour. Did he also know how close she had been to giving him total possession? A warm flush spread over her cheeks, and she saw the glimmer of amusement in his eyes. She realised that he knew everything.

She decided to leave the provocative question unanswered, and to give in gracefully instead. Rather retain her dignity than continue an argument which Eugène would end up winning anyway. She got to her feet, holding the letter to Marcella. She saw his eyes on it, and had a brief flash of amusement at the thought of what he would say if he knew to whom it was written.

'Don't be long,' he ordered.

'As long as it takes,' she returned, dancing him a saucy smile. He did not answer, and she was glad that for once she had had the last word.

The first time they had ridden together they had gone through farm-lands, and Eugène had combined pleasure with work. This time the black stallion led the way in a direction away from

Rusvlei and Hibiscus Vale.

Soon they were in open veld. The trail was narrow, and Eugène on the stallion stayed slightly ahead of the mare, so that Roumayne was able to watch horse and rider unobserved. As before, she noted how well they suited each other. There was the same sense of power and virility, the hint of ruthlessness, the sensualness that was as compelling as it was disturbing. There was no way in which she could have got out of riding with Eugène, short of an argument which she would not have won, but she was glad she had written to Marcella. Eugène's proximity played too much havoc with her emotions. The sooner she left here and regained her equanimity the better.

She willed herself to stop thinking of Eugène and to give herself over to the joy of the ride. Surprisingly, this was simpler than she had imagined. It was a blue and golden day. Wisps of white cloud floated in a clear blue sky, and a cooling breeze riffled through the thorn trees. On all sides stretched the bushveld, silent, brooding, mysterious, exerting the magic which never failed to move Roumayne.

The track widened, and Eugène slowed the stallion, allowing Roumayne on White Star to catch up with him.

'Glad you came?' he asked.

'Oh, yes!' For once she was able to talk to him naturally. 'It's wonderful out here.'

He did not answer, but the warmth in his smile

quickened her heartbeats. This was as she must remember him, Roumayne resolved. Tall and athletic, sitting so easily astride the powerful stallion, with the wind ruffling the dark hair, and the rare smile in his eyes. Today could well be the last day she would ever spend with Eugène. This was one picture she must keep in her mind. It would have to sustain her for many years—perhaps all her life.

They dismounted at a vlei, hidden and unexpected in the long grass. It was small, just a little patch of water, but it was fringed with willows and water-lilies and the sun splintered the water into a thousand diamonds. A kingfisher skimmed the surface, very near to three brown wild ducks.

'This is beautiful!' Roumayne turned an enraptured face to Eugène.

'It is,' he agreed mildly.

'Did . . . did you know it was here?'

'Of course,' he said, and then: 'Do you mind if we talk about something else, Marcella?'

Something in his tone took the rapture from her face. His eyes were enigmatic and unreadable. She was breathless all at once. 'Yes?' she whispered.

'I want you to marry me,' Eugène said quietly.

'What!' She stared at him through a blur, wondering if she had dreamed the words.

'I asked you to marry me.' His voice was very soft now.

'Oh, Eugène!' Luminous blue eyes gazed at him through a haze of pure joy.

His next words brought her back to earth with a very hard bump. 'I wonder why you're so surprised, Marcella?' A slight pause. 'After all, it's what you've been angling for all along.'

The haze cleared. For a few crazy foolish moments she had been overcome with a happiness she had never known before, believing it was her, Roumayne, whom Eugène wanted to marry. But of course, this wasn't so. It was incredible that she could have been so stupid! Eugène's proposal was directed at Marcella. The realisation struck her like a jet of cold water.

'That's right,' she said, and managed a brittle laugh. 'It *is* what I wanted, isn't it?'

'Then why are you so surprised?' The brown eyes studied her speculatively, curiously.

'Because ... oh, because you haven't been too enthusiastic about that matter until now, I guess.' She dropped her eyes, as much because she could not meet Eugène's penetrating gaze, as to hide the turmoil inside her.

'It's not only a woman's prerogative to change her mind.' A hint of hardness crept into his tone. 'You haven't given me an answer.'

What was she waiting for? This was the moment she had worked toward. She had written to Marcella, asking her to come back, knowing full well that when she left Rusvlei it would be without a penny. Now, in an instant, all had changed. Marcella would return to find herself engaged, and Roumayne would have the means to begin a new life.

Strange that the prospect of being penniless seemed more appealing.

During the night she had told herself that there could never be a future for herself with Eugène. That being the case, logic told her that she should be glad that at least she would be getting a reward for the task she had performed. But logic did not come into it. All she knew was that the thought of the selfish and mercenary Marcella getting married to Eugène was unbearable.

Eugène was waiting for an answer. She had no choice now, if indeed there ever had been a choice. There could only be one answer.

'I'll marry you, Eugène,' she said, as steadily as she could.

A hand went under her hair to her throat, coaxing her head up so that he could see the unshed tears in the amethyst eyes.

'You don't really want to marry me, Marcella.' His tone was gentle.

'I do. Really I do!' The touch of his hand filled her with despair. She tried to move from his grasp, but the hand on her throat was firm, and now his other hand went to her arm, beginning a soft stroking movement that sent flickers of fire shivering from her shoulder to the very tips of her fingers.

'Why are you so unhappy?'

Roumayne shook her head violently. 'I'm not unhappy.'

'Are you doing this to please your grandparents?' he persisted, watching her intently.

'Of course not.' She cast about in her mind for a way to change the subject. 'It's just.... Well, I must admit I'm puzzled. You ... you've said nothing about ...' she hesitated, then uttered the word, 'love.'

The stroking movement was halted. His laugh was mirthless. 'Aren't you pushing this a little, Marcella? First you try to persuade me into marriage. Now that you have what you wanted you ask me about love.'

'Why *have* you proposed, Eugène?' Curiosity emboldened her to meet the mockery in his eyes.

'That, my dear, is my business,' was the enigmatic response. A pause. 'Just as your reasons for accepting me are your business.'

What had brought Eugène to this point? Did it matter? Marcella did not love him, just as it was apparent that he did not love her. But each of the partners had reasons for wanting the union, and might in the long run derive from it what he or she sought. The poets would never call this a marriage made in heaven, yet, given the nature and the motives of the two people concerned, perhaps the marriage would be a success. For herself, Roumayne knew that she would rather remain alone all her life than enter into wedlock with such cold-blooded calculation.

The joy had gone out of the day. From the start she had known that Eugène could never be for her. Yet for a few seconds, when he had made the proposal, she had been so delirious with happiness that she had forgotten her role. Returning reality had brought with it disappointment and numbing unhappiness. The thought that Marcella would be the wife of the man Roumayne loved caused a blade of pain to twist in her chest.

When she got back to the farmhouse, she would open the envelope and add a postscript to the letter. With luck, the news she desired would bring Marcella home quickly. As far as Roumayne was concerned, the girl could not come soon enough. Every day that she had to prolong her stay at Rusvlei could only increase her unhappiness.

'Well, Marcella, shall we seal our betrothal with a kiss?' Though Eugène spoke with irony that was deliberate, his eyes held an expression which could not be equated with lightness. It was not love, nor was it mockery. It was an expression which Roumayne did not understand, yet which stirred her intensely.

For the moment she had no option but to go on with the farce.

'Of course we must seal it.' She looked up at him, coercing her mouth into what she hoped was a smile. She twined her arms around his neck in the parody of a happy fiancée. He must never know that the embrace, in its particular context, was pure torture.

His kiss was light, polite, totally devoid of any passion or tenderness. It occurred to Roumayne that Eugène, like herself, was performing a ritual for the sake of form; not because it was what he wanted, but because it was the correct behaviour in the circumstances.

Puzzled, she loosened her arms and tilted her head back to look up at him. She did not catch him off guard. There was nothing lover-like in the brown eyes that stared back into hers. They were sardonic and impenetrable.

'We both can do better than that,' he agreed quietly, in answer to her unspoken question. A gleam of mischief lightened his eyes, and the hint of a smile lifted the corners of his mouth. Roumayne knew he was remembering their shared passion of the previous night. She could not stop the warmth that stained her cheeks, nor the sudden trembling of her limbs.

When he spoke again his voice was low and seductive. 'I know this is just a formality, but shall we try it again?'

'You're so damn clinical about the whole thing!' The need to escape made Roumayne angry.

'A quality that you share, Marcella.' The brown eyes were teasing as Eugène took hold of her shoulders and pulled her to him. 'But it doesn't prevent us from enjoying each other.'

Unthinking, she tried to pull away from him. For the moment she was not Marcella, who had just become engaged, but Roumayne, who could not bear the indulgent amusement of the man she loved.

'No!' she exclaimed.

'Yes—my future wife.'

Amusement had vanished from his tone, to be replaced by command. No indulgence now in the arms which pulled her to him, fastening behind her back in a vice of steel. For a futile moment Roumayne still tried to avoid him, turning her head away from the descending mouth. But he was too quick for her. His lips clamped down on hers, and this time there was nothing tender or teasing in his kiss. As if to punish her for her attempt to escape him, his lips were merciless and possessive.

One hand began a slow deliberate movement along her back, sending a torrent of desire cascading along her spinal cord, drawing from her an ardour she had not known she possessed. The arms which moments ago had gone around his neck in an empty gesture, now went about him without volition, tightening compulsively as she pressed herself closer against him and gloried in the feel of the hard torso moulding itself against her softly feminine curves.

Fire rushed through her, scorching her with a heat that burned more deeply than the hot African sun overhead. Never in her life had she been so acutely aware of another person. Never had she ached to be so close … part of him. The pounding of his heart against her breast told her that he wanted her as much as she wanted him.

Rational thought ceased to exist. Later she was to wonder what would have happened if he had not put her away from him when he did. Trembling, she gazed up at him through a misty shimmer of tears. She loved him so much. Would she have had the strength to resist if he had insisted on taking the final step and staked full possession?

'I told you we could do better.' His voice was a warm caress, and he was still close enough for her to hear his heightened breathing, the strong beat of his heart. She could only look back at him numbly, unable to speak.

He gazed down at her, brown eyes holding blue ones with an eloquence which was unnerving. 'You were right all along, Marcella. At least this is one area in which we will be compatible.'

But we won't be. I'm not Marcella. I'm Roumayne, and I love you. But you'll be making love to a woman who doesn't even care for you, and who'll be replacing you in her mind with visions of her Frenchman. While I.... I shall be in some lonely bed-sitter, trying to find a job where nobody knows me, trying not to think of you, yet unable to make a life with anyone else.

In that moment Roumayne knew that what she had tried to fight had in fact happened. Eugène had destroyed for her any chance of future happiness with another man. She would have to spend the rest of her life alone.

'Shall we go and tell the news to your grandparents?' Eugène asked. His hand was on her arm, stroking it gently, seemingly unaware of the fresh fires he kindled inside her.

Roumayne nodded. Did it matter if he took her inability to speak as a sign of emotion? He would not know that the emotion he mistook for joy was in fact a numbing unhappiness, so intense that if she tried to speak she would cry.

They mounted their horses in silence. Once, as they rode back to Rusvlei, Roumayne found Eugène's gaze on her. In his eyes was an expression which he made no attempt to conceal. It was not love that she saw there, but a blending of curiosity and satisfaction—and something more. She caught her breath.

'I shall have to buy you a ring.' The words were unexpected. 'What shall it be?'

Roumayne closed her eyes for a second. In her mind she could see the ring she would want if she was in fact marrying Eugène. It was very old, made of silver filigree, with a glowing amber stone in the centre. She and Alec had seen one like it in an antique shop, Alec had not liked it. He had insisted on conforming with convention.

'A diamond?' Eugène prompted.

Roumayne opened her eyes. Of course! It had to be a diamond. Nothing else would please Marcella. Eugène was watching her, his expression polite and waiting.

'Naturally.' Roumayne's response was brisk. 'The bigger the better.'

His laughter rang out low and devastatingly seductive in the quiet bushveld air. 'You're a mercenary child, Marcella. Your grandparents think Paris has turned you into an angel. But you still run true to form, don't you?'

'What if I do?' Roumayne could not resist the

question. 'You still want to marry me?'

'Of course. I wouldn't have asked you if I didn't.' Mischief gleamed in the handsome face. 'Just don't make the mistake of thinking you've deceived me, Marcella. You haven't.'

But Marcella *has* deceived you. And so have I. You're in the grip of a deception you do not deserve.

In confusion Roumayne dropped her eyes, hiding them beneath thick silky lashes. How could she have let Marcella talk her into this dishonest farce? she wondered unhappily. Surely not even her pain after the trial should have allowed her to live a lie. She tried to remember the anger she had felt then, and the bitterness. Bitterness at a world which had not believed her, and a fiancé who could not live with that disbelief. A bitterness so intense that it had not occurred to her that by falling in with Marcella's scheme she would be wronging fine people.

Strangely it was a bitterness which now was hard to remember. Perhaps in one sense Rusvlei had healed her as she had hoped. That it would also be the scene of fresh unhappiness, lasting unhappiness this time, was something Roumayne had never foreseen.

'Having second thoughts?' Eugène's voice dropped softly in on her reverie.

'No,' she gulped, trying vainly to stem the tears which quivered treacherously beneath her lids.

The horses had slowed to a walk. Eugène reined in the stallion, and as if in answer to his command,

White Star stood still.

'Look at me, Marcella.' It was a quiet order.

Slowly she turned her head towards him. Time seemed to stand still while his eyes moved over her, noting the quivering lips, the pulse that beat too rapidly at the base of her throat, travelling upwards to her tawny hair, dishevelled where he had run his hands through it, and coming to rest at last on the tears which shimmered in the amethyst eyes.

Looking back at him, at the strong stern features in the lean tanned face, at the comforting breadth of his shoulders, Roumayne experienced a wild desire to throw herself into his arms and to confess.

The idea was as new as it was shattering. What would Eugène say? she wondered breathlessly. What would he do? She would start at the very beginning, and tell him all that had happened. He would hold her, and give her the comfort she needed so badly. And after that he would tell her that he loved her....

No! She shook herself impatiently, annoyed with her fantasising. For a variety of reasons she could not confess. As for Eugène's reaction to a confession, her dreams were nothing but wishful thinking. The reality would be anger—anger that he had been taken for a fool. Eugène's anger would be a terrible thing. And with it would come an icy contempt. No, Eugène must never discover the truth.

She was relieved when he did not comment on her tears. 'Let's go on,' was all he said quietly. 'Come along, dear.' There was something in his tone which made the endearment sound like a caress.

The grandparents were overjoyed with the news of the engagement. They plied the couple with questions to which Roumayne remained silent, letting Eugène supply the answers. There was a limit to which she could carry the deception. It was not possible to speak for Marcella on a matter which lay in the future, and which was so intensely personal.

But even without these scruples, Roumayne could not have spoken. Her own endurance had limits. The tears which had formed in the moments alone with Eugène were still unshed, hovering dangerously near the surface, fighting to overcome the forced smile she had fixed, as if with adhesive, to her face.

Just when Roumayne felt she could not bear the strain a moment longer, Eugène glanced at his watch and got to his feet. 'Time to go,' he observed. 'I have a living to earn.' He paused, and the look he sent Roumayne was wicked. 'More than ever, now that I'll soon have a wife.'

'Correct,' Roumayne agreed with an attempt at Marcella's cheeky flippancy. 'See you do it well.'

'Marcie!' Oupa's exclamation was shocked. 'That's a terrible thing to say to your fiancé!'

Eugène chuckled, unperturbed. A grin lifted the corners of his mouth, and his eyes were sardonic. 'Not terrible at all,' he reassured the old man. 'Marcella and I understand each other.'

He stepped close to Roumayne and put an arm

around her shoulders. Though she knew the gesture was meant for the sake of the grandparents, her heightened senses reacted to his closeness as they always did. She tried to block her mind to the consuming male virility of Eugène, and wondered if he felt the shudder which rippled involuntarily through her slender body at his touch. If he did, he gave no sign of it. He bent, dropped a chaste kiss on a hot cheek, and said, 'We'll choose the ring soon. Goodbye, my love.'

When Eugène had gone the excited grandparents wanted to talk some more, but Roumayne pleaded a headache and the need to be alone.

'This is a big day in Marcie's life, Jan.' Ouma sent Oupa a warning look when it seemed he was about to protest. 'It is understandable that she should want a little time to reflect.'

Reaching the sanctuary of her room and her bed, Roumayne gave way to the tears which had threatened for so long. She wept for Eugène, for the love which she had found, which she had won for Marcella and lost for herself.

After a while she left her bed. The tears had dried, and now she just felt numb and drained. In the bathroom she dashed cold water over her eyes and face. Then she slipped unseen from the farmhouse.

Making her way quickly through Ouma's tropical garden, Roumayne found the trail which had become her favourite. Leading away from the cultivated farm-lands, it wound up around the rugged slopes of a kopje to a small flat-topped plateau. Little grew in this rocky windswept spot, except for scrub and a few hardy thorn-trees. Roumayne had found the plateau in her first days at the farm, and was drawn back to it often, more especially when she wanted to be alone with her thoughts.

She sat down on a rock and gazed at the surrounding countryside. Below her lay the farm-lands. She could see the orchards of Rusvlei and the plantations of Hibiscus Vale. Deliberately she moved her eyes away from Eugène's lands, and gazed at the distant mountains, their slopes translucent and mysterious in the midday sun.

There was so much she would miss when she left Rusvlei. The loss of Eugène would be an aching wound which would take a long time to heal—if it healed at all.

But there was more she would miss. In the time she had been here, Roumayne had come to love Marcella's home, and had wondered often how the girl could have wanted to be away from it for so long. On long walks through the bushveld, Roumayne had absorbed much of its atmosphere. There was the ruggedness which had a beauty all its own. There was a sense of brooding and serenity; a sense of stillness. Above all the bushveld had a quality of infinity which gave a measure of comfort and reassurance to a troubled mind.

The midday sun was burning hot, but a slight breeze skimmed the plateau, ruffling the thorny branches of the acacias, and cooling Roumayne's perspiring body. It was quiet on the kopje, save for the incessant hum of unseen insects, a sound which was as much a part of the veld as the thorn-trees and the scrub and the sun.

In a few days Roumayne would be gone from here. It would not take Marcella long to get back. When she read Roumayne's postscript she would have all the incentive she needed to return quickly. It gave Roumayne no joy at all to know that she had accomplished her mission. The thought that Marcella would be Eugène's wife, sharing his name, his home, and—for she must face the bitter knowledge—his bed, brought her nothing but anguish. Perhaps if Eugène's future wife had been someone worthy of him, Roumayne would have found some consolation in the fact that at least the man she loved would be happy. But Marcella was shallow and calculating, wanting Eugène only for the material things which he could provide.

How astonished Marcella would be when Roumayne declined the promised rewards! It was only today, atop the lonely kopje, that Roumayne had made the decision consciously, but she knew that it had been in her mind for a long time. She would not accept a cent for her part in the engagement.

Life would be hard for a while, yet whatever the world might believe of her alleged negligence, Roumayne was a competent nurse. She would find a job in a place where she was not known, and her salary would be enough to support her. She would have to live carefully, but she would still have her self-respect. Self-respect was what she would lose if she were to take money from Marcella.

Thank heavens for her career, she thought. She knew now that she would never marry. She owed Eugène no loyalty, but it would be wrong to marry another man when she loved Eugène as she did. There would always be the temptation to compare, and it was unfair to expect any man to enter a marriage as the inevitable loser in that comparison. At least nursing was a rewarding occupation. She would give to it all she had. It was all that was left to her.

Roumayne was calm when she left the plateau. Decisions had been made, and she had come to terms with herself. If she could feel no happiness that was only to be expected. All she could hope for was that the time would come when her memories would provide a measure of peace.

She took the long way back to Rusvlei. On the main road was a post-box. Into it she dropped the letter to Marcella.

CHAPTER EIGHT

A RAY of sun caught the ring, and the diamond gave off a brilliance that was breathtaking. It was a big diamond, flawless and beautiful. Even without the help of the sun it had a radiance and life of its own. Sitting against a rock on the plateau, Roumayne lifted her hand and looked at the ring from another angle, intrigued, despite herself, by the dancing kaleidoscope of colours.

For herself, she would have preferred the antique ring of her dreams. But Marcella would be well satisfied with this diamond. Roumayne neither knew nor cared what Eugène had paid for it, but she realised that it must have been very costly. She knew, too, that to Marcella the ring would not represent a token of Eugène's esteem, but rather a promise of all the other worldly luxuries that would be hers in the future.

The thought of Marcella brought a frown to Roumayne's brow. What on earth was keeping the girl? She should have been at Rusvlei by now. Each day Roumayne waited for a letter, telling her when Marcella would arrive, and her plans for the way in which they would make the exchange. Ten days had passed since Roumayne had written to her, asking her to return—ample time for Marcella to have replied. That she had not done so made Roumayne wonder whether she had received the letter. She was beginning to think that perhaps Marcella and the gorgeous André had decided to continue their fling elsewhere. If that were the case, and if she had left no forwarding address, there was no telling when she would come.

Her eyes were troubled as she left the rock and began to make her way back along the trail to Rusvlei. The grandparents were giving a party to celebrate the engagement. In their excitement they had wanted to have the party sooner. Roumayne had done her best to try to talk them out of the idea of a celebration, but all she had succeeded in doing was to postpone it. Certain that Marcella would return quickly, she had been satisfied with the compromise.

But as the days passed and Marcella did not make her appearance, Roumayne grew worried. The thought of acting the part of a radiant bride-to-be was abhorrent.

Once, deliberately casual, she mentioned to Eugène that she did not think the party was a good idea, but he gave her no support.

'Nonsense, Marcella. You know how you love to be in the limelight,' he told her. His tone was teasing, but when she looked at him she saw that the dark eyes were enigmatic and watchful.

Not for the first time Roumayne wondered what there could be in this marriage for Eugène. Not love—that much was obvious. It could only be that by marrying a neighbour—for Rusvlei would almost certainly belong to Marcella one day—he would have the means of extending his own farm.

Often she wondered if he still saw Yvette Stacy, but she did not question him. When she had done so in the past he had been curt, contemptuous, making no secret of the attachment. Roumayne herself had not seen Yvette Stacy for some time. She did not know where they met, and when, but that was their affair, and she did not doubt that Eugène would be discreet about it. If she, Roumayne, had been the genuine bride, the situation would have been intolerable. She would not have agreed to the engagement without asking questions, without being certain that Eugène would stop seeing the other woman. But as it was, she did not care to incur Eugène's anger purely on Marcella's behalf. She had done enough for the girl. Marcella herself would have to deal with the matter of Yvette Stacy. Roumayne suspected that Marcella would not mind if her husband continued with his affair, so long as she could have her own freedom to live her life where and how she pleased.

The question of the party remained. After Eugène's teasing comment, Roumayne realised that she could not press the issue. It would not do to behave so out of character as to arouse his suspicions. And the hope remained.... Perhaps Marcella would return in time.

That hope was now gone. In a few hours the first guests would arrive, and Roumayne would have to play a double part. Not only must she be the radiantly happy girl who had just become engaged to the most eligible bachelor in the district. She must also be Marcella Du Toit, who had grown up at Rusvlei, and who had known all these people since childhood. One slip, one look of hesitation when she spoke to someone whom she did not know, but who had been a life-long friend of the family, and even the grandparents would become suspicious of her identity.

Panic welled in her at the thought of the ordeal. Did she have it in her to carry it off? A brainwave! She could pretend that she had fallen and had hit her head against a rock, resulting in a mild case of loss of memory. The idea was tempting, so very tempting.... But no, there had been too many lies already. Firmly she put the idea from her mind.

Her dress was lying on her bed. Roumayne and Ouma had driven into town to choose it. It was appropriate for a party in the garden, yet its simplicity was deceptive, for it was so well cut and flattering that Roumayne knew it was one of the loveliest garments she had ever worn.

When she was dressed she walked out on to the wide stoep of the house. It was still early, and the guests had not yet arrived, but a tall lithe figure stood at a table checking the drinks. At sight of him Roumayne's breathing quickened. His back was turned to her, and for a few moments she was able to watch him unobserved. Then, as if aware of her presence, he turned.

It was the first time she had seen him in a suit, and his distinguished appearance caught at her heart-strings. The suit was grey, well cut and expensive, and he wore it with the same ease with which he wore his casual safari clothes. He came towards her, a towering giant of a man, and she knew, even without seeing them, that Eugène Hugo would be the most handsome, the most impressive, of all the guests. She had a crazy wish to stretch up and run a hand through the thick dark hair, to trace her finger along the line of the mobile lips, those expert lips which had given her such torment and such delirious joy. But it was a wish she resisted, for she did not want to risk the consequences.

He was smiling as he said, 'You look extremely beautiful.' The words were banal enough in the circumstances, but there was no lightness in his tone, and the look in his eyes made it difficult for Roumayne to breathe.

Her chest constricted as those eyes, intense with an expression she had never seen, subjected her to a slow searching scrutiny. It was a scrutiny which took in every detail of her appearance. The lovely dress was moulded around the slim curves of the feminine figure. Narrow straps rested on smooth shoulders, and the low sweep of the neckline revealed the swell of softly rounded breasts. The amber shade of the dress enhanced arms and face turned a soft honey colour by the weeks of sunshine, and deepened the amethyst of eyes framed in long spiky lashes. Roumayne's cheeks were a becoming shade of pink, a colour which owed nothing to sun or artifice, but was brought on by the disturbing penetrating gaze.

'Extremely beautiful,' Eugène repeated slowly, in a voice that sounded a little husky. 'Come here, Marcella. I have something for you.'

'For me?' she whispered breathlessly.

'Who else?' He was smiling again, and this time the smile reached his eyes, lighting them with a warmth that brought a lump to her throat. He put his hand in his pocket, and drew out a long slender box.

He held it out to her. 'Open it, my dear.'

As she took the box from him, her eyes went up to his face. He met her gaze and held it for a long moment, a moment filled with a strange and sad eloquence that needed no words. She was the first to drop her eyes, unable to sustain the poignancy of that gaze any longer.

So chaotic were her emotions that her fingers trembled as she opened the box. A pendant lay on a bed of black velvet. The chain was of heavy gold, and on it rested a topaz. The amber-coloured stone glowed as if with a life of its own. It was the most beautiful thing she had ever seen.

Wordlessly she looked up at him, quite unable to speak. Her role was forgotten for the moment. She was Roumayne Mallory, and her heart was in her eyes.

'Do you like it?' His voice was not quite steady.

'It's ... it's exquisite,' she whispered tremulously. 'Eugène, it matches my dress. How did you know? Did ... did someone tell you?'

'I have no need to ask questions about you, darling.' It was the first time he had used the word, and it caught at her heart. 'Don't you know that yet?'

A happiness such as she had never experienced overwhelmed her. Then suddenly, with the cruel force of a body blow, memory flooded back. She had no place here. The pendant could not be hers, just as the man she loved more than life itself could never be hers. She hid her eyes to conceal the tears that shimmered on her lashes.

'Let me put it on for you.' His voice was low and seductive, and as he bent towards her, the clean warm breath caressed her cheek.

She stood very still as he clasped the pendant about her neck. For a long moment his fingers remained there, even after the pendant was secure. Ice and fire; the cold of the metal and the warmth of the fingers against her skin. A union which tingled with the vibrancy of electricity, producing an excitement which made it hard to breathe.

Without thinking she turned. His arms were waiting, and they closed around her as she buried her face in the fabric of his jacket. He wanted her as much as she wanted him—she knew it by the fierce beat of his heart against her cheek. She lifted her head and looked at him, then his mouth met hers in a kiss that was pure rapture.

The sound of footsteps brought them back to reality. Oupa had come on to the stoep.

'The first guests are here.' The weatherbeaten face was creased in a smile, and Roumayne knew he had seen the embrace and was glad of it. Over the weeks she had developed a strong affection for the kindly elderly couple. Sadly she hoped that they would never discover the truth.

'We're coming.' Eugène's arms still held her, and his voice was low. 'Ready, Marcella?'

'Yes.'

With more confidence than she felt, she smiled up

into the dark brown eyes which still glowed with rare warmth. He kept an arm about her as they walked to the wide stone steps, and all at once the confidence became genuine.

She would enjoy this evening, she resolved with a sudden flash of determination. No matter that she must play a part with people she had never seen and who were supposed to be her friends. She had managed until now. If Eugène and the grandparents were taken in by her act, then the guests would believe it too. This was her night, and she would enjoy it, all the gaiety and excitement of a party and, best of all, the attention of the man she loved. No matter that she was like Cinderella at the ball. At least when the time came to leave Rusvlei and to return to her own manner of cinders, she would have one more memory of a love that might have been hers if circumstances had been different.

The party was in the form of a braaivleis, and by the time all the guests had arrived and been welcomed, the fires were ready for the meat. Oupa and Amos had placed small barbecue stands about the lawn. The fires had been lit some time earlier, giving them time to die down a little so that the leaping flames would not burn the meat.

The braaivleis had the ingredients dear to tradition—great juicy steaks, crisp lamb chops, and Ouma's own home-made boerewors, tender and piquantly-flavoured. Mealies, hot to the fingers and dripping with melting butter. And afterwards, for all those who could manage a little more, there was

golden melktert, sweetly-rich koeksusters, and a
tangy piece of watermelon konfyt.

This was a braaivleis as it was meant to be, Roumayne thought, far from the noise and rush of the
city. Small coloured bulbs had been strung through
the trees to give light. The African sky was a brilliant mass of stars, the air was heavy with the mingling aromas of wood-smoke and roasting meat, and
above the talking and laughing of the guests rang
the song of the crickets.

Talking to people turned out to be simpler than
she had feared. The trick was to make no attempt
to call them by name, or to wonder who they were.
Sooner or later names came out of themselves, and
then, when she could, Roumayne used them naturally. Nobody seemed to notice that she was not Marcella. People were relaxed, happy, enjoying the excitement of the party.

Roumayne was talking to Tannie Elsie, a friend
of Ouma's, when Eugène appeared beside her and
put his arm around her shoulders. She smiled up at
him.

'It's good to see two young people so happy together,' Tannie Elsie observed. 'Have you set the
date for the wedding?'

'Not yet.' Roumayne spoke a little too quickly,
and was about to change the subject when Eugène
interposed calmly. 'We shall be married in a fortnight.'

Roumayne gasped with shock, and for a moment
she was unable to speak.

'So soon?' Tannie Elsie's eyes were narrow with suspicion.

'Of course not,' Roumayne managed to say firmly, as she recovered a little of her composure. 'Eugène is joking.'

'A fortnight,' Eugène repeated lightly. 'Either of you two ladies feel like a drink? No?' He grinned at Roumayne, his teeth a wicked flash of white in the firelight. Then, taking his arm from her shoulder, he walked away.

Roumayne watched him merge with the darkness. All the pleasure of the evening had vanished. Now she could only hope that the party would end quickly.

Ouma and Oupa Du Toit were philosophical about the matter. 'It doesn't give us much time,' Ouma conceded, ladling scrambled eggs on to the breakfast plates.

'It gives us no time at all!' Roumayne burst out unhappily. 'I won't do it!'

'I don't know....' Oupa's brow was wrinkled in a frown. 'Eugène must have his reasons.' The old eyes took on a sly gleam. 'I remember my own impatience when Ouma was my *nooi.*'

'Hush, old man!' came the pretended reprimand, but the old lady was smiling. 'We'll find a way to manage, Marcie. In a way....' She paused. When she continued, she seemed ill at ease. 'Well, perhaps it is for the best. I mean, we thought that perhaps you and Eugène would not get married at all.' Her eyes met Roumayne's steadily. 'Be careful, *kindjie*. Don't press him too much.'

The implication was clear. From the start Eugène had not been an ardent suitor. In fact his proposal, when it came, had been a complete surprise. If his fiancée now played the reluctant bride, he might well have a change of mind.

The grandparents were not to know that a change of mind was the very thing Roumayne wanted. And if not that, at least a lengthy postponement, long enough to ensure that Marcella would have returned to the farm.

'Won't the haste seem suspicious?' Roumayne asked tentatively. 'You should have seen Tannie Elsie's face when Eugène named the date. She all but asked me whether I was expecting a baby!'

The grandparents exchanged an uneasy glance, so that Roumayne wondered whether the same suspicion had been in their own minds. However, their granddaughter's reluctance for a speedy wedding would have been reassuring.

Ouma said firmly, 'You don't need to worry about Tannie Elsie, *meisietjie*. She would find gossip anywhere.'

'And the whole neighbourhood knows what a good girl you are,' Oupa backed her up stoutly. 'I agree with Ouma, *liefie*. If Eugène wants the wedding so soon, let it be that way. Sometimes I think it is best not to postpone things. At the moment Ouma and I are both well, but things can change.'

The nurse in Roumayne came quickly to the fore.

'Is something wrong, Oupa?'

'No, *liefie*, thank God there isn't. But we are getting old. Who knows what tomorrow can bring?'

There was nothing more Roumayne could say. But later, when Eugène fetched her to go riding, she turned the conversation back to the wedding.

'Why don't we wait a little?' she began uncertainly, trying to conceal the tension inside her.

'Don't you want to marry me, Marcella?'

His voice was so soft that she turned her head to look at him. There was power in every inch of the long lean body astride the black stallion, a power which was somehow enhanced by the easy, almost lazy manner in which he sat his horse. But there was nothing lazy in the appraisal of the dark eyes.

Roumayne had to force herself to look away from him, lest the sensual virility of the man swamped her senses to the point where she could no longer think rationally. Did she want to marry him? Yes! More than anything in the world. Treacherously there insinuated itself into her mind a picture of a tall lean man in a dark suit, beside a girl in a long white dress, with orange blossom in her hair and radiance shimmering in the amethyst of her eyes.

In an effort to banish the picture from her mind she shook her head vigorously. The action was not lost on Eugène

'You look like Don Quixote tilting at his windmills.' He laughed mirthlessly. 'I'd have understood a verbal "no" just as well.'

She looked at him in confusion, and then as she

realised that he had taken the physical action as the answer to his question, she coloured violently.

'No ... no, you're wrong.' The words emerged in an uncertain stammer. 'I ... I do want to marry you.'

'You have an odd way of showing it.' Sardonic amusement glinted in his eyes.

She bit her lip. She was getting deeper and deeper into a situation over which she seemed to have lost control. Did a drowning man experience similar sensations?

She took a deep breath in an effort to regain some measure of composure. 'You don't understand, Eugène.' Her voice was low and unhappy. 'Of course I want to marry you. But not so soon.'

'Give me a reason.' His voice was level.

'It's too quick.' She attempted the ploy she had tried on the grandparents. 'People will be suspicious. Tannie Elsie thought I was pregnant.'

His laughter was deep and hearty, the throaty sound of a man who was very amused. 'I hope Tannie Elsie knows how to count!'

Roumayne bit her lip. Unhappily her eyes slid away from his face.

'Now give me the real reason.' The mirth was still in his eyes, but his tone commanded an answer.

'I need a trousseau. Linen, and clothes, and things....' she said lamely. 'And a wedding needs a lot of organisation, Eugène.' She paused. 'Besides, we need time to get properly reacquainted.'

'Any other excuses you can dredge up?' he asked laconically.

Roumayne knew better than to answer. Unhappily she dropped her eyes. Somewhere there must be a way out of this mess. She must find that way before it was too late.

She let out a stifled gasp as a hand gripped White Star's rein, and an arm circled her waist to scoop her from the saddle. So swiftly had he moved that she had not even seen him dismount from the stallion.

'Eugène....' she began desperately, her mouth quite dry as he laid her on the ground.

'Shut up!' The words were an order, rasped out inches from her ear. 'You've given me all the reasons why we should wait.' A low chuckle. 'Remember when you set out to prove that I would want to marry you? Now it's my turn to prove to you why we should *not* wait.'

If he meant to rape her she did not have the strength left to fight him, Roumayne thought numbly, as the long hard body lowered itself on to hers. Or perhaps the truth was that she did not want to go on fighting herself.

He was tender, with a tenderness so seductive that it kindled in her an almost unbearable longing. There was nothing punishing in the lips that explored and teased, in the hands that opened buttons and pushed the blouse from her shoulders, then caressed the bare skin of her back and lastly her breasts.

She had meant, if not to fight, at least to remain passive. But she could not. With a moan she surrendered the will to resist. Sliding her arms beneath his shirt, she gloried in the muscles that pulsated through the strong torso, in the hair that was rough against the palms of her hands.

Tenderness vanished as his passion grew. He was heavy on her, vital and male and intensely alive. Her heart had been his for some time. Now, with every fibre of her being she yearned for him to possess her finally, in the way a woman is possessed by the man she loves. Right and wrong no longer entered into it. There was only the rough scrub of the veld against her back, the cloudless African sky above, and the vibrant body of the man she loved.

When he moved away from her she felt bereft. He sat up and looked down at her. His breathing was still uneven. 'Well,' he said mildly, 'I hope I've convinced you?'

She could only stare up at him wordlessly. But as he bent down and drew her blouse back on to her shoulders, fastening the buttons with an infinite gentleness, a shudder went through her, and she closed her eyes to hide the sudden rush of tears.

CHAPTER NINE

As the wedding preparations got under way, the quiet farmhouse became a hub of activity. Time was short and there was much to do. The ceremony was to be held in the garden at Rusvlei, beneath an archway smothered in a trailing cloud of mauve wisteria. Afterwards there would be a party. Nothing grand, just a tea to which all the farming folk of the district would be invited. It would be a simple affair, but one with warmth and dignity.

Ouma began to bake, cakes and biscuits and a fruit cake rich with nuts and raisins and sultanas, which later would be covered with a thick marzipan icing. Unhappily Roumayne watched as the old lady bustled about the kitchen with a vigour that defied her arthritis.

A dressmaker came out from Nelspruit, and Roumayne had to stand motionless while the woman pinned and snipped and moulded the white fabric of the wedding-dress to the soft curves of the slim figure.

As the wedding-dress began to take shape, Roumayne's despair increased. Still no word from Marcella, and with the wedding just a week away she felt as if she were in the grip of a nightmare which grew worse every day. Most nightmares end with the dawn, but this one seemed to have no end, no solution, no indication of when or how she would emerge from it.

No matter which way she looked at it, Roumayne could see only one solution to her problem—Marcella's timely return. And that now seemed unlikely. The day after the engagement party, when she had come back from the ride in the veld with Eugène, still dizzy from his lovemaking, Roumayne had despatched a telegram to Marcella. Almost a week had passed since then.

She could not remember a dilemma like this one. Even the court case, with all its unpleasantness, had not been so baffling. She had no clear idea what she should do.

The logical thing, the only thing, was to confess. But a confession meant unpleasantness. There would be the confusion and disappointment of the two elderly people whom she had come to regard with as much affection as if they had been her own grandparents. There would be Eugène's wrath. Much as she loved him, Roumayne quailed before the thought of his anger. It would be a terrible thing to experience. Lastly, there would be trouble for Marcella. Despite the girl's cold calculation, Roumayne had agreed to take her part, and therefore owed her some loyalty. Yet circumstances had taken a drastic step forward, and loyalty could not be put before dishonesty of such magnitude.

In euphoric moments Roumayne saw herself going through with the marriage. At those times she could see herself, a radiant bride in the beautiful white dress that had been especially made for her, going to join a tall figure beneath a wisteria-covered archway.

The day-dream never continued beyond this point. Reality would take over, and Roumayne would find herself faced squarely once more with her problem.

It was obvious that she could not go through with the marriage. That would be carrying the farce out of the region of calculated scheming into the type of wrong-doing which was not only immoral but illegal. The question was how to solve the matter in a way that would incur the least anger, disappointment and confusion.

At length she reached a decision. She would send one more telegram to Marcella. This time perhaps the girl would receive it and return, and they would effect their exchange. Marcella would wear the dress that had been made for Roumayne, and perhaps, since nobody had seen through the first step of the deception, they would be likewise blind to the second.

The episode would have a happy ending, at least as far as Marcella was concerned. For Roumayne it would always be a painful memory.

If Marcella did not react to the telegram, then there was no choice but to confess. It would not be possible to do anything else.

The issue in question was now only the timing of the confession. In fairness to Eugène and the Du Toits, Roumayne could not delay it much longer. On the other hand, if Marcella did arrive in time, everyone concerned would be spared much embarrassment and unhappiness.

And so Roumayne's own confusion continued and grew. At night her mind was a chaotic whirl so that she lay sleepless. During the day she moved about listlessly, frightened and unhappy. Though she tried to hide her feelings with a show of forced gaiety, she thought the grandparents guessed at her unhappiness. Now and then she caught them looking at each other helplessly. At such times she came close to hating Marcella.

If Eugène was aware that Roumayne was the antithesis of the joyful bride-to-be of tradition, he did not comment. In one sense Roumayne was glad. Eugène's lack of sensitivity would make the exchange relatively simple. But at the same time she could not help being hurt by his sheer indifference to her feelings.

It was on the day that she finally decided to make the confession that the letter arrived. She took it to her room and opened it with fingers that shook.

Marcella had scribbled it in great haste. The writing sprawled untidily over the paper, and Roumayne had to struggle to decipher it. It seemed that the circumstances had been more or less as she had imagined. Marcella and André had gone to Durban. On their return Marcella had found the letter and the telegrams.

The tone of the letter was one of arrogance. It seemed never to have occurred to Marcella that Roumayne might have difficulty in achieving her objective. What annoyed her was the fact that the wedding was to be so soon, necessitating an abrupt end to her 'bliss' with André.

Roumayne let the letter drop to the ground. Thoughtfully she stared out of the window. Marcella's selfishness appalled her. Then an idea entered her mind. Even now there was time to confess. Perhaps Eugène, furious that he had been fooled, would refuse to go ahead with the wedding. It was what Marcella deserved, and a fine tantrum she would throw if she returned to Rusvlei to find that she was not in fact about to become mistress of Hibiscus Vale.

The idea was tempting, so very tempting. But it was also impractical. The time for confession had long passed. By this time tomorrow Marcella would be safely ensconsed at Rusvlei, and Roumayne would be on her way to a lonely anonymity. Sighing a little, she picked up the letter and tore it into tiny shreds.

Grudgingly she had to admit that the other girl had laid her plans well. The exchange was to be effected with such shrewd simplicity that nobody would be aware that it had happened. Roumayne would leave before breakfast, unobserved. Very soon thereafter Marcella would arrive. Life at the farm would go on as it had always done. Nobody would ever know that a girl called Roumayne Mallory had spent both the happiest and the most miserable weeks of her life at Rusvlei, and that when she had departed she left behind her heart.

The rest of the day dragged interminably. Now that her departure was so near, Roumayne was oppressed with a sense of unreality. She was in limbo. She no longer felt part of Rusvlei, nor did she feel part of her new life—wherever that might be. For once she could not summon the strength to be gay.

It was during the afternoon, when she could not bear the strain any longer, that Roumayne decided to take a final walk to the kopje. On the windswept plateau she leaned back against a rock and gazed out over the countryside.

Her heart was as leaden as the grey sky overhead. Now that the time had come to leave Rusvlei, she did not know how she could bear it. It did not even seem likely that she would see Eugène again before she went.

A loud clap of thunder shook her from her reverie, and dazedly Roumayne looked around her. The sky had grown darker and the rough scrub of the kopje hissed in the wind. Roumayne shivered as she got quickly to her feet.

She realised now that even when she had left the farm there had been a sense of breathless waiting, the stillness of the birds and the dullness of the sky. All the signs of an impending storm. Knowing that a storm was likely to break, under normal circumstances Roumayne would not have been so foolish as to venture so far. But since the arrival of Marcella's letter her mind had been a mist of pain through which no external factors had penetrated. If she had noticed the dullness of the day, it was a dullness which had seemed to fit in with her own state of mind. She had been too preoccupied to question it further.

Lightning forked suddenly through the clouds, brightening the greyness over the mountains in a flash of white. Moments later there came the sound of the thunder, reverberating loudly through the stillness. At the same time the first drops of rain began to fall.

She was silly to be frightened, Roumayne told herself as she started down the kopje. True, the isolation and height of the kopje made it very vulnerable to lightning, but the storm was not yet overhead. She had learnt to measure the distance of lightning by the number of seconds which intervened between it and the thunder. However, it was not far away, and storms could be unpredictable in the speed with which they moved.

The rain grew harder. Another brilliant streak of lightning was followed almost immediately by an ear-splitting roar. Roumayne let out a cry of fear. The storm was travelling fast; now it was almost overhead.

She must get off the kopje quickly. Heedless of the stones which slithered underfoot, she began to run. And then, as her foot turned on a sliding stone, she fell. She struggled to get to her feet, only to fall once more when her left foot buckled under her weight.

Sobbing with fear and pain, Roumayne cowered

against the ground, pressing her hands to her ears to drown the merciless sound of the thunder. It was incredible that the storm had moved quite so fast. The rain lashed the earth in a fury, and the thunder was almost continuous, ear-splitting and terrible. Suddenly a blazing streak of orange shafted the high ground where Roumayne had been only minutes before.

At sight of the shaft which could have cost her her life, she was more frightened than she had ever been in her life. Without thinking she screamed, 'Eugène!'

'Idiot!' The word grated out harshly as strong arms lifted her from the ground and held her for a moment against the reassuring comfort of a broad chest.

Then he started with her down the slope.

'I'm too heavy for you,' she protested once, pushing her head back so that she could look at him. Rain streamed into her face, and she had to shout to be heard above the roar of the storm.

'Shut up and keep still!' The command rang out mercilessly.

She could not see his eyes, but his jaw was a long rigid line of strength, and above it his lips were pressed tight, either in anger or in tension. Even now, he was implacably in control. Thick dark hair clung wetly to his wide forehead, giving him an air of wildness. He was like some primaeval god of the storm, powerful and fierce and unafraid, utterly at one with the elements that raged about him.

Incredibly, Roumayne's fear vanished. A delicious sensuality swamped her senses as she lay back against him, her face nuzzling his chest. It was as if in his arms danger ceased to exist.

And then, quite suddenly, they were out of the rain, and when she looked around her she saw that Eugène had dumped her unceremoniously down on the floor of a small cave.

'I didn't know about this cave,' she observed wonderingly.

'Just as you didn't know better than to go out in a storm.' He glared down at her, his face a chiselled and unsmiling mask.

'I . . . I didn't know there would be a storm.'

'There's no end to the things you didn't know.' The ghost of a smile touched his lips. 'Strange that, my dear. This storm has been brewing all afternoon.'

Roumayne watched silently as Eugène shifted dry leaves and twigs into a mound. He seemed to have lost all interest in her, now that they were out of danger.

'How did you know where to find me?' she asked him after a while.

'I took a chance. Oupa Du Toit thought you'd gone for a walk. Since your return from Paris,' he paused, and there was an odd gleam of malice in the glance he shot her, 'the kopje seems to have become your favourite haunt.'

'Anything wrong with that?' she defended herself tautly, aware that her heart was pounding. 'The view from the plateau is so lovely. As I'm an art student, why should you wonder that I go up there for inspiration?'

'Perhaps I would wonder less if you took your paints with you.'

The words were said lightly enough, but Roumayne eyed him sharply. What had he meant to imply? Perhaps nothing, for Eugène seemed to have lost interest in the conversation. He drew a match-box from a plastic wrapping and set a spark to the dry twigs. Soon a tiny fire threw a thin light against the rock walls of the cave.

Gratefully Roumayne spread her hands to its warmth.

'Get your clothes off.' The order was light.

She jerked her head up, swiftly, questioningly.

'I said get your clothes off.' He sounded impatient. 'They're soaking wet.'

'I ... I can't,' she stammered, and felt the blood pounding in her temples.

'Why not?' For a moment he seemed genuinely puzzled. Then he chuckled. 'Are you going to be a shy bride, Marcella? I find that hard to believe after all the proof you've given me of our physical suitability.'

'Do you need to be obnoxious?' Roumayne spoke very quietly to hide the quiver in her tone. His words had hurt her, bringing back the realisation that she would never be Eugène's bride, that she would never know his love in the way she most wanted. 'I can't stand, Eugène. I've twisted my foot.'

'Badly?'

At the unexpected concern in his face she could only nod her head.

'I should have known.' He laughed softly. 'You're no helpless ninny to lie waiting for help when you could have been running back to the farm on your own.'

As he talked his hands loosened her sodden sandals. Then he began an examination of the injured foot. For hands so large, so vitally male, they had a great gentleness. Even through Roumayne's pain, his touch on her skin was like a caress.

'It's not serious,' Eugène pronounced at length. 'By tomorrow you'll be walking on it again.'

'Tomorrow?' The word jerked out of her in horror as she remembered all that was to happen the next day. She struggled up. 'But, Eugène, we must get back to Rusvlei today!'

He glanced at her curiously, as if he wondered at the desperation in her tone. Then he said lightly, 'We'll go when we can. But we must wait for the storm to end.

'Yes....'

It was strange how his presence had made her forget the storm. Outside the rain still hurtled down in tropical torrents, and the thunder rolled and crashed. The cave was small but dry, and the fire gave off a light that was comforting.

'Let's get your clothes off now.'

Eugène's tone was matter-of-fact and impersonal, but Roumayne's fingers had gone suddenly nerveless, so that she could only fumble helplessly at her buttons. His hands nudged her fingers away. As gently as he had examined her foot, he now removed her garments. She did not try to stop him. As a nurse, she knew only too well the dangers of remaining in wet clothing for too long. As a woman she knew the dangers of being unclothed in the presence of the man she loved.

'Don't,' he said softly, when she covered her breasts with her hands.

In response to the husky request she removed her hands slowly. Her shyness was replaced by a sweet and nameless longing. She knew that if Eugène wanted to make love to her, she would let him.

She sat quite still as his eyes lingered on the rise and fall of her soft breasts, smooth as pale ivory in the light of the fire, then moved upwards to the slim pulsing throat, and further to the tremulous lips and eyes which were bright with unshed tears. Her heart thudded violently in her rib-cage, so that she thought he must surely hear it, but pride stopped her from lifting her hands to her body again.

For several seconds that had no meaning in time, his eyes worshipped her. 'You're very beautiful,' he said, and his voice was so low that she wondered if she had imagined the words. A shudder went through him. Then he took off the sweater which had stayed dry beneath his raincoat, and lowered it over her head. She turned her face away to hide an aching disappointment.

The fire began to die. There were no more twigs in the cave, and it grew very cold. Outside the storm still raged, and Roumayne knew there was no question of leaving the cave yet. It had grown dark. She did not have her watch with her, and could only guess at the time.

'My grandparents will be worried,' she said tentatively.

'They'll realise that I've found you.' Eugène's tone was self-assured. 'Let's get some rest.'

She lay back against the rocky ground, her face once more turned away from him. Eugène lay down close beside her, and she felt her muscles tense as his arms closed around her.

'We've got to keep each other warm.' His breath was clean and caressing against the back of her throat.

'Is that the only reason why you're so close to me?' She could not resist the question.

'Witch! Don't you know that's a leading question?' He chuckled softly. 'You know what I want. But we've a lifetime of loving ahead of us, my lovely bride-to-be.'

His arms tightened around her, so that she could feel the whole long length of his body against hers. Consuming tongues of desire raced through her, sending the blood pounding through her veins. She was about to turn to him, when the arms loosened their hold slightly.

'Let's keep it this way.' The warning came huskily. 'In less than a week we'll be married. Let's wait till then, sweetheart.'

They lay quite still in the darkness, and after a while Eugène's slow steady breathing told Roumayne that he was sleeping.

She could not sleep so easily. A lifetime of loving, Eugène had said. The words burned like a brand in her mind. His arms were still around her, holding her close. To him, the gesture was no more than a sensible precaution—mutual bodily warmth to guard against the risks of exposure. But to Roumayne, their lying together was sweet agony. She was vibrantly aware of the hard sleeping body. She could feel the muscled thighs, taut even in repose, the strong rhythmic beat of his heart. His arms were against her breasts, and his breath stirred the tiny hairs at the back of her neck.

A lifetime of loving.... Lying like this, in an intimacy which was almost unbearable, Roumayne could imagine so well what it would be to be Eugène's wife, to lie at night in the circle of his arms, fulfilled and content, knowing that years of loving and sharing stretched ahead.

Eugène would have Marcella. If that girl responded to his lovemaking with Roumayne's ardour, her husband might never know that for a brief period of time there had been another girl in his life. But for Roumayne, the years that lay ahead looked barren and very lonely.

She did not know that she grew tired. It was only

when Eugène shook her awake that she realised she had slept.

For a few seconds she did not know where she was. She was confused as she stretched her stiff limbs and shivered in the chill air. Then, as her vision cleared, everything came back to her. A pale grey light filtered into the cave, revealing the remains of the little fire, and when she looked up she saw Eugène standing over her, his lean features looking more rakish than ever beneath a fine covering of hair.

And then the grey light, which could only be dawn, took on a stark relevance.

'What time is it?' she asked, her throat dry with anxiety.

'My stomach says breakfast-time.' His grin was teasing.

'Heavens!' She was appalled. 'We've got to get back.'

'So we will.' He was studying her with an intentness which belied the nonchalance of his words. 'Do you never say good morning when you wake up, Marcella?'

'What?' She stared at him blankly, her mind reeling at the thought that she might not be able to effect the exchange in time. Even now Marcella would be on her way to Rusvlei.... 'Er ... yes. Good morning, Eugène.' The words tumbled out unsteadily. 'We must hurry. Please!'

'We can only go as fast as your foot will allow.'

The rejoinder was placid. 'Let me look at it, Marcella.'

Long fingers took hold of her foot, probing with gentle expertise. It took all of Roumayne's will-power to maintain an outward appearance of calm. Her heart raced with fear.

'The swelling has gone down.' He straightened, satisfied. 'And your clothes are dry. Right, Marcella, let's go. But take it easy. The foot might not stand up to another fall.'

Even without Eugène's warning, Roumayne soon realised that it was necessary to go slowly. The trail down the kopje was slippery after the rain. Stones had been dislodged, and roots were strewn across the path. Once she slithered on a muddy patch, but Eugène shot out an arm, saving her from a fall.

'I said take it easy.' Brown eyes gleamed a warning.

Looking up, Roumayne caught her breath at the slow thoughtful gaze flicking her face, a gaze which registered lips quivering with tension and eyes blurred with fear.

His feet were planted slightly apart, his legs braced against the slippery mud of the trail. He towered above her, a lean tanned giant of a man, exuding an aura of strength and authority and control. The rugged features were stern, the dark eyes impenetrable. A little desperately Roumayne searched his face for warmth, and found none. Perhaps it was his relentlessness which gave her the illogical impression that he knew the motive for her haste, the reason for her fear. Then she shook herself impatiently. It was her own feelings for the man which endowed him with an insight which he could not possibly possess.

They did not speak as they continued down the trail. It required all of Roumayne's concentration to negotiate the mud and loose stones. Now and then she cast a glance at the eastern horizon, where the sun was beginning to lift itself from the land. The sight ceased to fill her with despair. All she felt now was numbness, a dreadful sense of being a puppet moved by the strings of destiny, unable to manipulate any longer a situation which seemed to have slipped beyond her control a long time ago.

The sun was quite high when they reached Rusvlei, and through the air wafted a thin smell of cooking. Roumayne's inclination was to slip in through a side entrance, but Eugène's hand was on her arm in a grip which allowed no defiance as he steered her towards the kitchen door.

Roumayne managed to be slightly behind him when they came through the door. Though the scene which met her eyes was the one she had expected, she was momentarily overcome by a wave of giddiness.

Sitting at the breakfast table before a plate of eggs and bacon was Marcella. As planned, she had evidently gone first to her room and donned one of the cotton dresses she had lent to Roumayne. The girl was so like her that it seemed to Roumayne as if she looked at her own image in the mirror—just like that first time, in the flat in Hillbrow, only then her unhappiness had prevented her from spotting the likeness. No wonder, she thought now, that nobody had seen through the deception. The only thing missing was the diamond ring. That was still on Roumayne's finger. Marcella must be wondering where it had been put for safe-keeping.

Marcella looked up and saw Eugène.

'Hello, darling.' Her smile was so casual that Roumayne had to admire her brazenness. 'I hadn't expected you so early, but I'm happy that. . . .'

The words tapered off as Eugene moved, and for the first time Marcella caught sight of Roumayne. For several seconds the scene in the kitchen seemed suspended in a petrified moment of time. Marcella's mouth was wide with horror. The faces of the grandparents were studies of disbelief.

Then, as if someone had released the catch on a movie-projector, everyone moved and talked simultaneously. Only Eugène stood quietly apart, his eyes sardonic and mocking.

'Marcie!' Ouma's face was distressed as she turned to Roumayne. 'Where have you been? And who . . .'—she looked at Marcella—'who is this?'

'*I* am Marcella.' The girl at the table leaped to her feet. Her eyes were blazing as she came to Roumayne, her mouth twisted in a dangerous snarl before which Roumayne took a step backwards. 'What are you doing here?' she hissed. 'You were supposed to be gone!'

'I . . . I was stranded in a storm.' The words came

out jerkily, Roumayne's chest so constricted with tension that it was an effort to speak.

'Stranded! You did it on purpose. You little bitch!' Marcella was about to hit Roumayne when Eugène caught her hand.

Suddenly Roumayne was very angry. 'Don't call me that again,' she said clearly.

'I'll call you what I damn well like!' Marcella was too furious to care what she said. 'You planned to get stranded.'

'Please.... We don't understand....' Ouma and Oupa were close beside them now, their kindly faces pale and distraught. Again Ouma asked Roumayne, Marcie, who is that girl?'

Marcella whipped around. Her voice was shrill. '*I* am Marcella. This'—she pointed an accusing finger—'is an impostor. Her name is Roumayne Mallory.'

'Is that true?' Oupa's voice was very low.

'Yes. I'm so terribly sorry....' Roumayne's heart went out to the elderly couple as she saw the intensity of their distress.

'It's a bit late for that. Give me my ring, and then clear out of here,' Marcella ordered.

Roumayne was about to comply when Eugène spoke for the first time. 'No!'

The word was said very quietly, but it brought a hush to the room. Roumayne turned, puzzled, as Marcella spun round to face him.

'You don't understand, darling.' It amazed Roumayne that the other girl's mood could change so rapidly from one of vituperative fury to one of seductive indulgence.

'I think I do.' The same mild conversational tone.

'That's my ring she's wearing,' Marcella accused.

'Is it?' The question was all the more dangerous for its quietness.

'Well, of course.' Marcella was impatient. 'I can explain everything, and I will. It's a damned nuisance that Roumayne messed things up this way. But it really doesn't change anything. The ring is mine.'

'I gave it to Roumayne.'

Roumayne caught her breath. It was the first time Eugène had used her real name, and despite the hopelessness of the situation, it sounded very sweet in her ears.

'I know that, darling, but it was a misunderstanding.' Marcella laughed gaily. 'It's quite a joke really. I'll tell you the whole story when we're married.'

'You don't seem to understand, Marcella.' Eugène's voice was sleek and smooth as a panther's. 'There's no joke.' He paused and smiled. 'I gave the ring to Roumayne. And we'll be married on Saturday.'

'What!' The two girls exclaimed the word together, Marcella in shock and disbelief, Roumayne in wonder.

Her heart was racing violently, and her eyes as she looked up at Eugène were misty with joy and love, revealing her feelings more clearly than speaking could have done. Involuntarily she turned her gaze to Marcella, wondering how she had taken the announcement.

Marcella's face was a mask of anger. Blue eyes glittered like marbles in a white face. Roumayne stared transfixed as the expression was replaced by a smile of pure malice.

'So, Eugène, you think you'll marry Roumayne.' The words dropped from her tongue in a soft and deadly poison. 'It's my duty to tell you that you'll be the husband of a murderess.'

'No!' Ouma's gasp was disbelieving.

'Yes. She murdered....'

Roumayne did not stay to hear the rest. With a little cry of pain she ran from the kitchen. As she left the farmhouse and began to make her way down the drive, as fast as her strained foot would permit, she was barely conscious of the tears that streamed down her cheeks.

It was enough that she had lost the man she loved. Till now there had been the hope that if ever he found out about the deception, once his initial anger had passed, he might remember her with some affection. Marcella's revelation had put paid to that hope.

How different was Marcella's attitude just now from the evening when they had discussed her scheme. When Roumayne had asked if she was not concerned that a girl of her reputation would be living in her home, Marcella had laughed and said,

'For heaven's sake! I've never doubted your innocence.'

The words had suited her purpose then, just as her malicious outburst in the farmhouse kitchen suited her now. Marcella would always behave selfishly, Roumayne realised sadly. The girl was entirely without scruples.

The fallen petals of the jacarandas were thick underfoot, a slippery mauve carpet which softened all sound. Until a strong hand caught at her waist she had not been aware of following footsteps.

'Eugène!' The name emerged on a dry whisper as he turned her round to face him.

'I didn't spend the night in a blasted cave just so that you could run hell for leather on that injured foot.' The warmth in his eyes belied the brusqueness of his words.

'You....' She moistened her dry lips with the tip of her tongue. 'You shouldn't have followed me.'

'No?' An eyebrow rose in sardonic amusement.

'No.' She was able to speak more firmly. 'You're only making it more difficult for us both.'

'You're wrong, you know.' Something in his tone set the adrenalin pumping through her system. Roumayne looked up and saw the smile that curved Eugène's lips and brought warmth to the brown eyes.

'Why?' A breathless whisper.

'If you'd run off I would have had to search for you.' The lightness in his tone was betrayed by the look in his eyes. 'But I'd have found you in the end.'

He paused and cupped her chin with one hand. 'Surely you know that, my darling?'

She could only shake her head wordlessly. Amethyst eyes were bright with tears, and a hard lump in her throat impeded her speech. At last she managed to whisper, 'Back ... back there in the kitchen you ... you said. ...'

'I know what I said, darling.' His voice was very soft, and the endearment had a tenderness which sent fresh tears shimmering down flushed cheeks.

'You couldn't have meant it.'

'Every word. I want to marry you.'

'I don't understand....' She gazed at him, heedless of her tears, of the fact that her heart was in her eyes. Somehow it did not seem to matter.

'Is it so difficult?' An arm went around her waist. 'I love you, Roumayne.'

'No!' The tears fell freely now as she buried her face against the warm skin of his chest, bare where his shirt buttons were open. He held her close, caressing her arms, her shoulders, kissing her ears and the top of her hair.

Presently she pushed herself from him. 'Didn't you hear what Marcella said? About me being a murderess?'

'You've never murdered anyone in your life,' he said matter-of-factly.

'That's true,' she acknowledged. 'I haven't. But, Eugène, you can't marry me. In the eyes of the world I was only acquitted for lack of proof.'

He shook his head. 'There's something you

should know, Roumayne. A week after you left your home someone came forward with the real story of what happened the night Jackie James died. Your lawyer tried to find you, but you'd vanished.' He paused and smiled. 'Your name has been cleared, darling.'

She stared at him, trying to absorb the full implication of what he had said. At last she asked, 'If this is true, how do you know it?'

'I made it my business to find out.' He laughed at her puzzled expression, then went on. 'There had to be a reason why a girl like you would agree to pose for an unscrupulous child like Marcella. I knew you'd lived in Johannesburg. Remember when you let that slip? I thought a deception could work both ways. I took a picture of Marcella to Johannesburg, and began my detective work. Once I went to the press it became easy.'

'So that's why you went away!' she exclaimed. And then, 'Eugène, when did you realise that I wasn't Marcella?'

'Almost right away. Never try to be an actress, Roumayne. You're a good nurse, but you'd fail on the stage.'

'The grandparents believed the act,' Roumayne said hesitantly.

'I know that. Bless them, they were so happy to see Marcella that they were quite content to put down all the nice changes in personality to a miracle that happened in Paris.'

'Was it the slip about Johannesburg?' Roumayne

was curious. 'Was that how you guessed?'

'I knew long before that. You made so many slips, darling. You were so efficient when the man was injured in the fields—Marcella can't stand the sight of blood, didn't you know?—and then you nearly fainted at the sight of a little grass snake which any country girl could have told at a glance was harmless.'

'So that's when you knew....'

'No, Roumayne, I knew the first day.' Eugène's voice was edged with amusement. 'Do you really think a man can hold a woman in his arms and not know that he'd never held her before? Especially'—he grinned wickedly at the warmth that stained her cheeks—'a woman as responsive as you?'

'And all the time I thought I had you fooled.' Roumayne smiled ruefully. 'Will the grandparents be very disappointed?'

'A little. But they had to learn the truth about their granddaughter some time. We spent a few minutes talking—that was why I didn't catch up with you right away. Darling, they want us to go ahead with the wedding just as it was planned.' He paused, and his eyes were lit with a warmth she had rarely seen in them before. 'If you *will* marry me?'

Jewel-like, the amethyst eyes spoke their joy. But there were still two things she had to know.

'What about Marcella?'

'When I left she was throwing a tantrum,' Eugène said crisply. 'That young lady wouldn't have suited me, Roumayne. Not under any circumstances. I've known that a long while.'

'I see....' She hesitated, for the second question was harder. She met his eyes levelly and asked, 'I'm sorry, Eugène, but I have to know—what about Yvette Stacy?'

'She left the scene a long time ago.' The eyes that met hers were steady.

'She went to Johannesburg with you?'

'Yes, darling, she did. Just for the ride. She'd decided to live there after I told her that I couldn't see her any more.'

'Why did you tell her that?' Roumayne was a little breathless.

'So many questions!' he mocked her gently. 'I broke with Yvette the day after I held you in my arms the first time. That was when I knew that there could only be one woman in my life.'

When he went on his eyes were alive with a rare warmth. 'You still haven't given me an answer darling. May I be the man in your life?'

'The only one,' she whispered joyfully. 'Now and for ever.'

And as she lifted her head for his kiss she knew that dreams really do sometimes come true.

Poignant tales of love, conflict, romance and adventure

Elegant and sophisticated novels of
great romantic fiction . . .
12 all-time best-sellers.

Join the millions of avid Harlequin readers all
over the world who delight in the magic of a
really exciting novel.

**From the library of Harlequin Presents all-time best-sellers—
we are proud and pleased to make available the 12 selection
listed here.**

Combining all the essential elements you expect of great
storytelling, and bringing together your very favorite
authors—you'll thrill to these exciting tales of love, conflict,
romance, sophistication and adventure. You become
involved with characters who are interesting, vibrant, and
alive. Their individual conflicts, struggles, needs, and desires
grip you, the reader, until the final page.

Have you missed any of these *Harlequin Presents...*

Offered to you in the sequence in which they were originally printed—this is an opportunity for you to add to your Harlequin Presents . . . library.

This elegant and sophisticated series was first introduced in 1973, and has been a huge success ever since. The world's top romantic fiction authors combine glamour, exotic locales and dramatic and poignant love themes woven into gripping and absorbing plots to create a unique reading experience in each novel.

You'd expect to pay $1.75 or more for this calibre of best-selling novel. At only **$1.25 each,** Harlequin Presents are truly top value, top quality entertainment.

Don't delay—order yours today

Complete and mail this coupon today!

ORDER FORM

Harlequin Reader Service

In U.S.A.:
MPO Box 707.
Niagara Falls, N.Y. 14302

In Canada:
649 Ontario St., Stratford,
Ontario N5A 6W2

Please send me the following Harlequin Presents...I am enclosing my check or money order for $1.25 for each novel ordered, plus 49¢ to cover postage and handling.

☐ 127 **Man in a Million**

☐ 128 **Cove of Promises**

☐ 129 **The Man at La Valaise**

☐ 130 **Dearest Demon**

☐ 131 **Boss Man From Ogallala**

☐ 132 **Enchanted Dawn**

☐ 133 **Come the Vintage**

☐ 134 **Storm Flower**

☐ 135 **Dark Castle**

☐ 136 **The Sun of Summer**

☐ 137 **The Silver Sty**

☐ 138 **Satan Took a Bride**

From time to time we find ourselves temporarily out of stock of certain titles. Rather than delay your order we have provided an alternate selection area on this form. By indicating your alternate choices, we will still be able to provide you with same day service.

Number of novels checked _____ @ $1.25 each = $ _____

N.Y. and N J residents add appropriate sales tax $ _____

Postage and handling $ __.49__

TOTAL $ _____

ALTERNATE SELECTIONS ☐ ☐ ☐

NAME _____
(Please Print)

ADDRESS _____

CITY _____

STATE PROV _____ ZIP POSTAL CODE _____

Put more love
into your life.
Experience the
wonderful world of...

Harlequin
Romances

Written by world-famous authors,
these novels put at your fingertips
a fascinating journey into the
magic of love, the glamour of
faraway places.

Don't wait any longer. Buy
them now.

Do you have a favorite Harlequin author? Then here is an opportunity you must not miss!

HARLEQUIN OMNIBUS

Each volume contains 3 full-length compelling romances by one author. Almost 600 pages of the very best in romantic fiction for only $2.75

A wonderful way to collect the novels by the Harlequin writers you love best!